Altered Reality
The Exceptionals Book 3

Mary Terrani
Sarah Cass

Urban Fantasy

Sarah Cass
www.authorsarahcass.com

Divine Roses Ink Publishing
www.divinerosesink.com

Other Books by Mary Terrani

Decking the Halls

The Exceptionals
Escaping Humanity
Chaos Theory

Books by Sarah Cass

The Tribe Series
The Tribe
The Wolf
The Chief
The Raven
The Dominion Falls Series
Changing Tracks
Derailed
Dark Territory
Runaway Train
Home Signal
The Lake Point Series
Santa, Maybe
Deep-Fried Sweethearts
Stalled Independence
Witch Way
A Thorough Thanksgiving
Eve's New Year
Heartstrings & Hockey Pucks
Luck of the Cowgirl
Stars, Stripes & Motorbikes
Free Falling
Love for Hire
Haunted Hearts
Stand Alone Novels
Masked Hearts
Leap
The Exceptionals
Escaping Humanity
Chaos Theory

Dedication
For Mary Terrani

Sarah,

We made it! Thank you for going on this journey with me. All the ups and downs and everywhere in between. Love you.

To Scott

Thank you for always pushing me and never allowing me to give up. Thank you for dealing with the many nights watching TV while I wrote. For knowing when to push me harder and when to make me stop and take a break. I love you.

To Ryan and Patrick,

Never give up on your dreams. Never stop being who you are. You have both turned out to be amazing men and I am proud to be your mother. Love you to the moon and back.

Dedication
For Sarah Cass

This book is for the one person without whom it never could have happened -
My best friend, Mary.

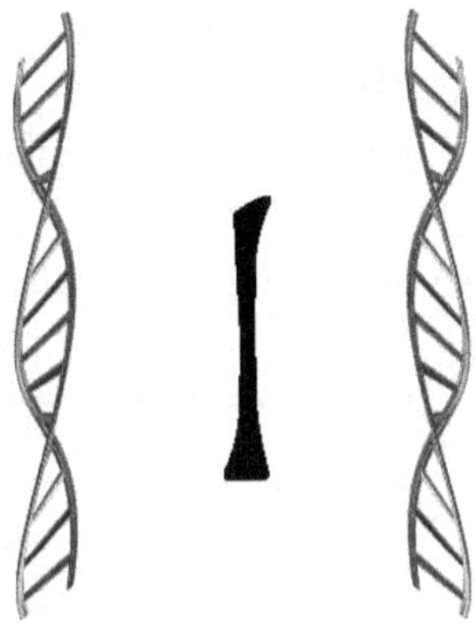

"Warren created a virus to try and kill me."

The sentence echoed through Abby's brain on an endless loop. Warren created a virus to kill their daughter? It couldn't be true. It had to be a mistake.

Warren's anger over losing Annie had been palpable. There wasn't a soul at the compound that hadn't been aware of it. He loved their daughter. He wanted her back in their lives. It couldn't be otherwise. No logical reason existed that he would have tried to not only hurt their daughter but murder her in cold blood.

"Mom?" The tremor and croak of Annie's voice matched the emotions Abby could feel pouring from her daughter. Nervous and raw.

"There has to be a mistake." Abby's voice squeaked the protest her mind had been spinning over and over. "Warren wouldn't do that. He's been angry, I know, but he loves you, Annie."

"I'm sure there's an explanation. Somehow. I'd peg Steele for something like this. Not Warren." Waves of uncertainty emanated from Talisa despite her best effort to stave off the coming chaos of emotion over Annie's declaration.

A trickle of blood slipped down James' arm where Annie clung so tight to him that her nails broke the skin. The usually temperamental James didn't even flinch. If anything, he held the trembling Annie closer to him.

Annie shook her head. "I know what I saw. It was his—"

"Anne?" James pulled back, tilting Annie's chin up. "Ma, something's wrong."

"She's in so much pain." Abby stepped to the other side of the table as she opened herself to more of the emotions in the room, specifically Annie's. She pushed a wave of calm toward the couple. James' gaze snapped toward her, but she didn't flinch. "Easy, Annie. Let Tal and Roark take a look."

"I—I—I—" Annie stuttered over the word as her whole body spasmed in apparent pain.

"Let's have a look at her." Roark moved Abby to the side with a gentle touch.

"James, you stand at the head of the bed so you're still close to her. Your bond can help her as much as we can." Talisa redirected her son, an intense expression darkened features.

Abby moved closer to Annie's feet. The Warren situation would have to wait in favor of helping Annie deal with whatever was going on. Talisa and Roark needed to ensure she wouldn't lose her daughter again. "Tal, what can I do?"

"Keep pushing the calmness, Abby. I know it may not seem like it, but it is helping." Talisa smoothly reconnected monitors in tandem with her husband, like their forced separation had further cemented their bond Tal continued speaking in quiet tones to Annie. "Slow down. We're going to figure out what's going on. Focus on James."

"Her vitals are all over the place," Roark murmured.

The moment James' hand broke contact from Annie to maneuver to her head as instructed, an ear-piercing scream cut through the room as Annie's back arched off the bed.

The daughter Abby had just gotten back was in agony, and there wasn't a damn thing she could do about it. The scream cut off suddenly when Annie collapsed back onto the bed--eyes closed and breathing shallow.

"Anne!" James lunged forward but stopped at a glare from his mother. After a brief moment where they stared at each other, James' hand settled on Annie's forehead. Tal gave him a curt nod.

Talisa remained silent while she examined Annie. Heart, lungs, pupils, the basics. "She's in shock. Roark."

"On it." Roark already had the bag of lactated ringers in his hand.

"What could have caused that?" Abby reached for her daughter's leg to offer more direct comfort but hesitated in fear of causing more pain.

"Any number of things, but if I had to hazard a guess, I think she came out of the chamber way too fast." Talisa nodded in Roark's direction a split second before he injected something into the IV.

"Ma." James' forehead rested on Annie's now, his voice raspy and shallow. "She was terrified. I don't mean scared; I mean full blown terror."

"We won't know anything for sure until she's awake again and we can talk to her." Roark jotted notes down on a pad. "Right now, your mom is talking to her, but not about that."

Abby was a doctor. She knew what every beep from the monitors meant, what every readout said, as well as every look Talisa and Roark exchanged. None of it was good. Nothing at all pointed toward the positive. "How long should she have been in the pod before she came out?"

"At least an hour. Once she reconnected with her body everything needed to reboot—so to speak." The briefest twitch of a smile crossed Tal's lips at the small pun, but it was gone in an instant. She pulled her hair loose, but immediately swept it back into another ponytail. "She had to fully integrate with her physical form. Annie flew out of there in less than five minutes. Brain, organs, all the way down to her skin needed time to adjust to having someone in charge."

"We're giving her fluids and electrolytes to get her started. We'll run some blood work and see if there is anything else her body is missing. She'll wake up once her body adjusts." Roark moved the IV pole closer to the unit and hung another bag of fluid, so it was ready to go.

"Come back to me, Anne. You promised." James' thumb brushed along Annie's jaw line. He didn't move to get any closer, remaining at the head of the bed while his parents worked.

"Do you really think Warren could have anything to do with something so heinous?" Abby worried her bottom lip between her teeth.

"I don't know." Talisa finished her examination. "Her blood pressure is beginning to stabilize. That's a good sign."

Abby took the chance to grasp Annie's thigh. "I can't understand."

Talisa blew out a long breath. "I don't want to speculate, Abby. We need to focus on getting Annie through this first. Then we can look at the rest of the matter."

"I know. You're right. You're right. I just…" Just what? If what Annie said was right, she needed to get her family as far away from the man she married as possible. Lock him up in a cell like they should have done after he'd attacked James and Elan."

"Whoa, Ab. Not prying, but you're projecting pretty hard there." Talisa pulled Abby into a fierce hug. "I promise you we'll get to the bottom of this. If Annie's correct, then we *will* get him locked up tight."

Abby soaked up the comfort offered in her best friend's tight hug. "Thank you. I need you to promise me something."

"Name it."

"When we do address it, don't let me do something I'll regret."

"If I must do it for you, I will. Spirits know, I don't regret."

Ilana sat slumped on the edge of the bed. In her hands she held the cursed scroll her mother had given her. It seemed entirely ridiculous. Tal didn't need to worry about Ilana's problems in the middle of the latest crisis to befall the group.

Never ending crises.

Again, and again.

Crisis, rinse, repeat.

"It's all a load of bullshit," she muttered to the empty room.

She unfurled the scroll carefully. It might not be quite as old as dirt, but it was at least as old as the tribe. Painted in surprising detail and color was a figure. A figure that, according to everyone remaining in the tribe, was her.

The Guardian.

Protector.

White wings spread wide; her face upturned. Short hair floated on a current of air. Even the clothes seemed modern.

The door slid open in a soft hiss and Ilana released her hold on the skins. The scroll rolled back into shape without a whisper of sound.

Ethan had stopped moving as soon as he'd entered the apartment. Had he sensed her presence, even without telepathy or animalistic senses?

"Lana?"

She smiled at the nickname, relieved he wasn't too angry with her. So much of her struggle she had kept to herself so she couldn't blame him if he had been angry. "I'm here."

"Thought you might be." He paused in the doorway to lean against the frame. He seemed a little rough around the edges for some reason. Hair mussed, collar crooked.

Ilana's sharp nose caught a whiff of stale moonshine. "Were you drinking?"

"Yesterday. You smell that?"

"Dude. I smell everything it seems like. We all do."

"Right. Sorry. Meant to shower" He paused for a beat.". Danny's in crisis."

Of course, he was. Wasn't everybody? "Shocking."

He tilted his head. "You ok?"

"Nope."

"Want to talk about it?"

"Yes, and no."

The right side of his lip quirked in a hint of a smirk. "That's helpful."

"What would be helpful is if you showered. Moonshine is not a good cologne."

For that, he laughed outright. "Fine. If I shower, will you want to talk about it?"

"My answer won't change, but I will talk about it."

"Give me five minutes."

"Better make it ten. I swear you bathed in that shit." She managed to find a smile of her own to compliment his warm laughter. Knowing he wasn't upset with her helped. She'd kept silent far too long, but it wasn't like he didn't know she was having nightmares. Or something like them.

While she waited, Ilana brewed a pot of tea. Anything to distract her from the near incessant thoughts in her head. At least she could turn off the telepathy, unlike her brother and mother.

"It is time, yet you resist."

Ilana blinked in the bright sunlight that suddenly appeared. A figure walked her way, silhouetted against the sun. The voice, neither male nor female, gave her no insight to who it was.

At the same time, she swore she'd heard it before.

"Who are you? What do you want from me?"

"You already know. You've always known."

"If I knew, I wouldn't have asked." Ilana growled low.

"You know."

She only knew what she yearned for, "Set me free."

"We are trying." The figure rushed forward. A high-pitched scream rang through her senses as the fingers closed on her shoulders.

"Ilana!" Ethan shook her by the shoulders.

The high-pitched whistle of the kettle filled the room. She shook herself back to the present. "Damn it." That had been the scream in her vision. The kettle, not the...what, or who, had it been?

Ethan's brows knit in deep concern. "What was that?"

"What?"

16

"You were—I mean—what *was* that?"

Ilana stared at him in confusion. His continued wide-eyed silent freak-out made her insides twist nervously. She grabbed the kettle to occupy herself. "What are you talking about?"

"You were only partially here."

"Stop the dramatics. My mind wandered."

"No. I mean it. Physically you were only partially here. You were part here, part phased, and half…half fucking invisible."

"Invisible? Ethan, really. Don't screw with me. I *wanted* to talk to you."

"Well now you're gonna *have* to." He took the kettle from her to set it back down. "I'm not screwing with you. Your face was your natural form. You know, the one you don't let anyone see but me?"

She knew all too well. Her natural state was not human. At least not as far as regular human flesh went. Her skin was a deep, rich brown—which would be fine if not for the odd black bumps and stripes that accompanied it. The whole thing had a weird way of making her look both animal and human. The yellow eyes didn't help matters, either. "You mean my Skinwalker appearance."

"You're not a Skinwalker," he muttered. His annoyance made his tone gruff as it always did when she derided her natural form. "That is an old tale of magic from years past."

"And now we regularly do what would have once been considered "an old tale of magic". I look like a Skinwalker, you can't deny it. I would be banished if the tribe was still strong and saw me in my natural form. Hell, I *am* a Skinwalker. I am able to shapeshift, remember?"

"Ilana, don't change the subject to pick an old argument in an attempt to distract me from what just happened."

She huffed in what she hoped sounded more like annoyance than amusement.

"As I said, you were partially in that form. Yellow eyes, dark forehead, but your lips and neck were like they are now. You were phasing out, though. I mean seriously. It looked like you were being beamed up to the *Enterprise* or something.

Ilana sank into the closest chair worried that her legs wouldn't hold her. Flashbacks to the tunnel meeting with Inessa flashed through her mind. "Inessa said she couldn't see me."

"What?"

Things were so much worse than she'd ever imagined. "Sit, Ethan."

"Lana?"

"I think…"

Ethan settled into the chair beside her. His warm hand rested on hers, making her aware of how cold she'd become. "What is it?"

Her throat constricted around the words she feared saying but knew she must. She forced them out in a raspy whisper. "I think they want to take me."

"What? Who?"

"The Spirits."

"Why?" Ethan's hand squeezed hers. "Why would they want to take you?"

"To punish me. For my innumerable failures."

"That's not true, and I'm pretty sure that's not how any of this works."

"Well, I don't know anyone else, besides me, that's failed to save thousands of lives before. I have."

"Lana."

"I'm going to let them have me."

18

Ethan's finger tucked under her chin, drawing her gaze to his. "Back up, baby. Back way up. Start from the beginning."

"The beginning?"

"Yes."

"I failed. That's the beginning. And the end."

Talisa rubbed her fingers along her forehead. Annie's revelation had sent everyone into a tailspin. With her telepathy still pretty fresh, such sudden and raw emotions were bombarding her already overworked brain.

"Li. Focus on me." Roark's voice calmed all the others. The simple nudge had her doing exactly that.

She offered him a brief smile of appreciation. *"Cans open, worms everywhere."*

"Leave it to you to quote Friends.*"* His deep chuckle rumbled through her mind.

"Hey. Friends *kept us laughing when we couldn't talk like normal human beings. If it works, it works."* She felt her smile grow more genuine.

"We got this." He squeezed her hand as he stepped up beside her. With a gentle tug, he pulled her flush against him. *"We're together again. With our family, we can get through anything."*

"Even one of our own losing his shit?"

"How many times did I lose mine when I first became an Exceptional?"

20

"Both of us did. Damn animal instincts."

"I like your animal instincts." He nuzzled her below the ear.

"Down, boy. Too much to do right now. Soon, though."

"Soon is never soon enough."

Tal had to force herself not to laugh out loud. He had a point. Then again, perhaps her promise of soon wouldn't be kept. With a heavy sigh, she squeezed his hand. *"I should catch Chance up on this latest development before he hears it from someone else."*

Roark tapped her hip. *"I'll keep an eye on Annie. Do what you need to."*

She turned to give him a proper kiss. "I'll be outside," she said to the room at large.

He winked and pinched her ass. "We've got Annie. See you in a few."

Tal slipped from the room into the hall. The hiss echoed through the partially built hallway. She stopped right outside the door, breathing out some tension. Though instinct alone told her Chance was near, she pulled her full attention away from her husband to seek out her best friend. Just as Roark's brain had been as familiar to her as he himself was, Chance's proved the same.

A calm pool amid the chaos, just like the man. *"Sani? Can you come down to the new lab?"*

"Everything okay, Kajah?"

"Yes and no."

"Sounds ominous. I'm on my way, not far away. Did something happen with Annie?"

"You could say that, but it's better to tell you in person." She tugged the hairband from her hair. The locks, which had become crazy long in captivity cascaded down her back. She

massaged her fingers over her scalp to ease some of her tension. It didn't work, but it was worth a try.

"Just the look on your face tells me something isn't right." Chance's features were etched in concern as he approached.

"I swear the worry lines on your forehead tripled while I was gone."

"The news that bad?" He placed a kiss on her forehead.

Tal closed her eyes, wishing she could delay spilling the truth. Waiting never did any of them any good, though. Instead, she blurted the whole thing quickly. "Warren tried to kill Annie with a virus while she was in transit back to her body."

"Just like ripping off a band-aid." Chance raked his hand through his hair. "Fuck. Are we sure? I mean, I know Warren was pretty pissed about not getting the laptop, but to kill her?"

"Annie is absolutely certain. She forced herself to wake up far quicker than she should have to get away from the virus. She was terrified." She folded her arms across her chest. "A year ago, I would have doubted it. From what we've seen since we've been back? I just don't know."

"Why kill his own daughter? It makes no sense." Chance paced along the hallway.

"We can add it to the list of questions we already have. I thought we'd have more time to figure out what was going on with him, but then this."

"We're out of time."

She blew out a frustrated breath. "Did anything happen while we were gone?"

"No. Nothing remarkable." He paused, leaning against the opposite wall. "The changes didn't start until after we retrieved Annie. It's like a switch flipped and he focused all his anger on your family. I don't get it."

"None of us do. We need to figure out what's going on with him before anyone else gets hurt."

"You're right. I hate it, but you're right. We need to contain him. I'll get RB and the others to start searching. How are James and Abby holding up?"

"Abby's crushed, obviously." She glanced toward the closed doors. "We're waiting until Annie wakes again to get more information, but Annie was pretty clear. James is wound tighter than a spring. He's waffling between wanting to tear Warren to shreds and begging the spirits for Annie to wake."

"Wait. You said Annie told you. Does that mean she's awake?"

"She was, but she dragged herself out of there far too soon. Her body went into shock. Vitals are stabilizing, but she hasn't woken back up." Tal bit her thumbnail, her gaze fixed down the hall as though all the answers sat waiting for her there. "You're telling me Warren was himself until Annie got here. What could have caused the change?"

"No idea."

She looked up toward the ceiling, wishing with her whole heart she was in the woods of their homeland carrying on this discussion. If she were honest, they'd gone from one prison to another. Though it might be for their protection, hiding under the surface away from fresh air and sun felt like captivity. She closed her eyes again. "What was Warren like around her?"

"When she first got here, he spent most of his time looking to see if she was a plant. He didn't trust it was real. She swore she wasn't one. Lucas helped her with a meditation that made her able to separate the implanted memories from the real ones. Once he stopped searching, he spent time with her like she'd always been here."

"I guess we can't blame him for thinking she was a plant."

"No, but Abby wanted him to just accept her so they could be with their daughter. He finally did, but then the whole mate thing came up. That's when he started to push against things with James." Chance frowned at the ceiling. "It was like the idea of her having a connection with James threatened his connection with her. Not even Charlotte pointing out their bond helped."

"All of this almost sounds like a trigger, which Steele loved to implant. It couldn't be, though. Ariel and Lucas cleared everyone when we first went into hiding." She buried her face in her hands. "This is one hell of a mess."

"It sure is. He's, our friend. Our family. But we can't have him attacking people in the compound. I should have ordered him to be put in containment when he attacked Elan and James. Maybe then we wouldn't be where we're at now."

"We can't think like that. The man is connected to computers, he could have done this damage from anywhere. Besides, we needed his help with the pod. Annie was running out of time. Everything is happening according to the Spirits plan. We may never know what that plan is, no matter how much we might want to." Talisa wrinkled her nose. "I sound like my father."

Chance's hearty laughter filled the corridor. "It's not a bad thing to sound like him, Kajah. I find any day that I sound like any of our parents, it's probably a good thing. I've thought of them often in the past year and asked for their guidance."

"Did it help?"

"When I stopped and listened to them, yes. Even though you were gone I had mini versions of you advising me. Lucas sounds a lot like your father most of the time."

"Li, Annie is holding steady, but Abby looks like she's about to rattle apart." Roark's voice filtered in hesitantly as if worried he'd interrupt.

"Be right there." Tal pushed off the wall. "Let's check on Abby. She needs us."

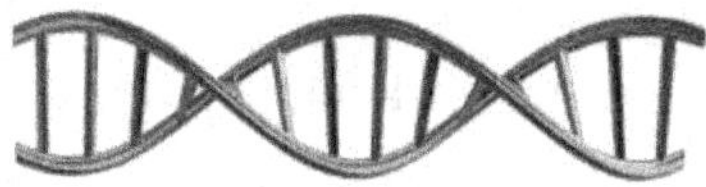

"Lana," Ethan spoke into the lingering silence. "I thought you were going to talk."

Ilana's entire being tensed under the gentle admonition. Though she'd started, forming the words proved infinitely difficult. "I..."

For several long minutes, Ethan waited her out. When she still didn't finish, he broke the silence again. "You aren't sleeping well, and you keep waking up in pain."

"Wait. Why didn't you say something if you knew that?"

He pressed his lips to her forehead. "Because I know not to push you. If I had, you would have shut down and told me nothing. You only talk about things when you're ready."

"You make me sound like the Spirits and their annoying cryptic messages."

He chuckled softly. "You are not annoying. Well, not all the time."

She smiled dutifully as expected at his joke. It faltered nearly as quick as it had formed. She wrapped her arms around herself as if to hold the information inside. Lucas had pushed the information out of her against her wishes, but that was her brother. She should be able to talk to her husband. "I think the Spirits are trying to take back what they gave me—and kill me."

Ethan pulled back to look at her with such intensity she had to turn away. "What makes you think that? Everything I've heard from Lucas, Chance, you—hell, any of you—is that the Spirits are not like that."

"I told you; I shouldn't be the Guardian. I failed our people. I failed the Exceptionals. I failed my family. I failed everyone." Tears burned at the back of her throat.

"Lana." He dropped to his knees in front of her, clasping both of her hands. "Babe, look at me. You failed no one."

She sobbed as he tugged her into a tight hug. "All those people died under my watch. I failed, and now they're punishing me for it." A heavy weight settled in her chest, making it hard to breathe.

"Ilana Abigail Johnson. You listen to me, and you listen good." He grasped her shoulders, giving her a gentle shake. His gaze settled on her, firm and loving at the same time. "You did everything you could and saved everyone possible. You failed no one. Now tell me what exactly is happening."

Tears streamed down her cheeks unbidden. It didn't matter how much faith Ethan had in her. She knew she'd been responsible. "The visions are breaking me. Literally. I wake up with broken bones. Cuts, burns, tears in my skin. All healing as I come awake."

His lips pressed together in a thin line. "How does it happen?"

"I knew you wouldn't believe me." She sobbed into her hands.

"Hey, hey." He brushed a thumb along her cheekbone. "Don't do that. I've seen some pretty weird and fucked up shit since we all grew up at an accelerated rate. Hell, my sister died and jumped into a computer, remember?"

She nodded at her lap, unable to lift her gaze.

"I believe you. I'm just asking you to explain it to me, so I have the full picture. Tell me about one of the visions."

A shudder coursed through her at the thought of explaining yet again. Her voice shook as she spoke, "In the latest one I was like a balloon. Floating high above the earth near the clouds. A string tethered me to the ground below. Once I realized my wings weren't out, I crashed to the ground. It felt like my whole body broke. They keep saying I'm fighting what I am."

"Fighting what you are?"

"Yes."

"Okay, so you are floating until you realize your wings aren't out." Ethan's forehead puckered. "When you think you can't do it, that's when you crash?"

"Yes," her voice broke.

"What if it's as simple as believing in yourself? I mean, I know I'm not the smart one in the relationship here, but what if you don't need the actual wings? Maybe you can fly without them."

"What? Are you insane? Fly without wings? I can't fly without my wings."

"Have you tried?" He took her hands in his again, pulling them close to his chest. "I'm serious, Lana. Think about it. When you were helping me get a handle on my gifts, I could barely change the temperature. Then you suggested I throw a snowstorm; not just affect the weather around us. I told you it was impossible, but you kept on me and told me to believe in myself. Eventually I listened to my brilliant, beautiful wife and I did it. You believed in me enough until I could do it for myself."

"Ethan, this isn't the same thing. No one was trying to kill you while you were trying to do that." Ilana pulled her hands free of his. He didn't understand. No one could. None of them had been expected to be the Guardian.

"Eh, I'm pretty sure my parents wanted to kill me when I blew the windows out of the safehouse we were staying in at the time."

"I'm being serious."

"So am I."

"You don't understand. No one does. I fall every time, and it's going to kill me eventually."

"But what if you didn't?"

"Didn't what?"

"Fall. What if you had faith in yourself and didn't fall?"

Chance followed Talisa into the new lab. He didn't understand how the lengths Steele had gone through to hurt the Exceptionals could still surprise him. Yet it did, nearly every day.

The pods along the walls were a testament to how far the man would go. Steele was willing to not just kill them, but experiment on them. Hopefully it was in the Spirits plan that the ones they'd rescued would be able to join their group once Tal and Roark cleared them.

"Chief." Roark nodded in Chance's direction before turning back to the notes he was jotting on a clipboard.

"Abby." Chance wrapped his arm around the woman to pull her close. "How are you holding up with all of this?"

"Chance, I…" Abby's body shook against his with quiet sobs.

"Don't. Don't do this to yourself. We'll figure it out. We always do." He comfortingly ran his hand along her back.

"If Annie's right, he tried to kill our daughter." Abby's whisper shook with her emotions.

He cast a concerned glance at Talisa. "We'll find out what happened and how to help him."

"He's right. Let's take it one thing at a time. What do we always say?"

"One day at a time." Abby hiccupped softly.

"One day at a time, one hour at a time, one minute if that's what we need. We always get through. For now, we'll focus on Annie." Tal squeezed Abby's shoulder.

"We'll have to get Warren into a containment cell." Chance pursed his lips at the shudder that ran through Abby. "As a precaution. We'll get to the bottom of this and get your husband, and our friend, back."

"So, we need him back?" James piped up from his spot next to Abby.

"James," Chance said in a warning tone. "I understand you're upset, and understandably so, but we need to find out what happened before we act rashly."

"Sorry," James muttered with a good amount of contrition.

"James is right." Abby tried but didn't sound much stronger than she had a moment ago. "If we get to the bottom of this and it was all him? I don't know that I'll ever be able to look at him the same again."

"Something is wrong with him," Roark interjected. "When we were working on the pod together, he wasn't acting at all like the Warren I've worked and fought beside all these years."

"Virus," Annie's weak whisper interrupted them.

"Anne." James kept her hand in his as he focused his attention back on her.

"Don't push, Annie." Talisa touched Annie's leg gently. "We're all here. Give your body time to realize someone is in charge now."

30

Chance hugged Abby tighter. "You all take care of Annie. I'll see about finding Warren, and we'll go from there."

"Thank you." Abby wrapped an arm around him to hug him back.

"Tal, keep me updated. I'll let you know what I find out." He gave Talisa's shoulder a gentle squeeze as he walked by.

The door hissed shut behind him gently. Outside of the room and away from Abby's side, Chance released a smidgen of his control to unleash a heavy sigh. He scrubbed his hands over his face. "Spirits help us."

On instinct, Chance started toward his meditation room. Mentally he reached out to the other two telepaths. *"Lucas, Ilana, meet me in my meditation room please."*

"I am on my way, Ravenhawk," Lucas' voice filtered into his mind. He didn't get a response from Ilana but knew she would be there as soon as she could.

Once he reached his meditation room, he pulled bottles from the shelves out of pure muscle memory. He tossed a few herbs into the mortar and ground them with the pestle.

"Chief?" Ilana's voice came from the door.

"Ravenhawk." Lucas walked up behind her. "What can we assist with?"

Chance paused his grinding of the herbs when he took note of Ilana's features. The young woman seemed deeply troubled. Perhaps he shouldn't have called her. Still, they needed all hands-on deck. With a sigh, he turned back to his task. "I need your help in locating Warren. We need to get him into containment."

"Is this because he attacked Elan and James?" Ilana moved deeper into the room, pausing several feet away.

"I wish it were that simple, Illy." Chance turned around to face them. "Annie believes that Warren tried to kill her with a virus while they were bringing her back."

"They were successful in their attempt though." Lucas took Chance's place at the table, working the herbs in his place. He grabbed another bottle from the shelf to add to the mortar.

Chance allowed a brief smile that Lucas had selected an appropriate herb, although not one Chance's own first instinct had called for. Though the young man was the embodiment of what a Medicine Man should be in temperament and spirit, he still held some of his mother's outside-the-box thinking. "Yes. They were successful, but due to the attack she came out of the pod earlier than she should have. They're monitoring her."

"And I'm guessing we have no idea where Warren is at the moment." Ilana's frown deepened as heavy sarcasm laced into her tone. "Because nothing can be that easy."

"At the moment, no. We have no idea, and due to his gift, he has access to all the computer systems. We need to get him into containment until we can figure out what happened." Chance leaned against the table. "I should have let you mix the herbs to begin with Lucas. That will be better for Annie."

"You have many things on your mind, Ravenhawk." Lucas' tone wasn't placating, even as he made excuses for his Chief. As soon as he'd finished, they poured them into a tea ball.

"Who knows about this? It's going to kill Ethan." Ilana shoved her hands in her pockets, her glare focused on the bare floor.

"Abby, James, Annie, and your parents know. Of course, now the two of you as well. I need to talk to RB as well, but the faster we find him the better. I don't want to alarm too many people." Chance closed his eyes against the burgeoning headache that ached behind his right eye.

32

"We promise to be cautious." Lucas' calm tone remained beside him.

Chance inhaled a deep breath, then let it out slowly. When he opened his eyes, surprise startled him so much he rattled the table with how fast he pushed off. "Ilana?"

"She's right there," Lucas said quietly, still pulling herbs from the shelves.

"No, she's not. Where did your sister go?"

Lucas turned to search the room. "She was right there."

"What the hell?" Chance went on high alert. He scanned the room for any clue as to where she'd gone. He knew she could shapeshift, but there was nothing else in the room but them. In a fit of possible madness, he waved his hand where she'd been standing. It was a desperate hope that one of her gifts had malfunctioned and she'd merely gone invisible.

Nothing.

"I do not have a sense of her anymore. It is as if she is just gone."

Talisa's voice entered his mind with perhaps a hint of panic, *"Sani."*

"Crap. Your mother noticed." Chance pondered what to tell her. Then again, maybe she had more news instead of noticing. *"Yes, Kajah?"*

"Where the hell did my daughter go?"

"I don't know. She disappeared. We were talking. I closed my eyes for a minute and when I opened them, she was gone." Chance pinched the bridge of his nose. Like they needed another complication.

"If Mother noticed she is gone, then I do not believe it is an issue with one of her gifts," Lucas offered. Perhaps trying to be helpful, even if he failed.

"Why can't the crises come one at a time?"

Talisa left the room in a bit of a hurry. Tal's panic had been notable, so Abby kept her mouth shut to let them deal with whatever had arisen now.

Abby rose from her spot beside Annie's bed. James remained on the other side of her daughter, holding her hand. "James? Did you want something to eat?"

"I'm not leaving her." A low growl carried through his statement.

"I appreciate that." She didn't flinch as his growl deepened when she set her hand on his shoulder. "You need to keep your strength up for her. Healing or not, you require sustenance."

"I'm fine." James didn't move an inch, his gaze fixed on Annie.

Charlotte entered carrying a tray laden with food. "You need to eat too, Aunt Abby."

"Thank you, Charlotte." Abby forced a smile. Last thing she wanted to do was eat, no matter that she'd just been trying to push food on James.

Charlotte set the tray down. In the midst of her movements to unload everything, she gave Abby's arm a gentle squeeze. "How are you holding up?"

"Not good. After this morning I feel like I'm waiting for the other shoe to drop. For something else to go horribly wrong. I..." Her breath hitched into another blasted sob. "I don't understand how Warren could do this to our daughter."

"I'm so sorry, Aunt Abby. I don't understand it either. He was acting weird when he was working on the pod." Charlotte set a plate with a sandwich and some fruit in front of Abby.

"None of this makes sense. I can only hope there's no side effects from Annie coming out of the pod early." Abby picked off a piece of the sandwich to pop in her mouth.

"I think she'll be okay. Her body just needs to adjust. Once everything is done rebooting, she'll wake up." Charlotte set a plate next to the unusually still James.

Alarms blared through the room, startling both women.

"Annie!" Abby jumped up to move towards the monitor. "Everything looks fine here. Why is there an alarm going off?"

"It's not Annie." Charlotte moved closer to the bed where the little girl lay. "It's her."

Abby ran over and picked up the pad. Her whole body shook like she might lose it at any moment, and perhaps she would. If she could help, she needed to. That much kept her going. She'd not really done even basic medical care since Annie had died, but she certainly hadn't forgotten it, she'd been a doctor for years. "These readings all over the place. I don't see any root cause, though. It's like everything's going haywire. Blood pressure, heart rate spiked. Her oxygen levels have dropped. What in the world? She's in a medically induced coma. None of this makes sense."

"That seems to be the norm lately." Charlotte scanned the pad in her own hand.

Abby moved to one of the cabinets. She withdrew some phenobarbital into a syringe. "If we don't get her vitals back in line she's going to crash."

"How do we fix it if we don't know what we are dealing with?" Charlotte shone a pen light in the girl's eyes. "I don't understand it. It's like she's waking up."

"Which is why I'm putting her back under." Just as suddenly as they'd started, the alarms ceased. All readouts returned to normal.

The second the adrenaline stopped; Abby crashed to her knees with a deep sob.

"*Abby*," James and Charlotte yelled in unison.

Charlotte rushed to Abby's side. "Easy. It's going to be okay."

"How?" Abby managed to choke out the word before the next sob hit. She took a deep breath. "How is any of this going to be okay? Annie is still unconscious. My husband will be hunted down for trying to kill our daughter. Being around him and the pure rage coming from him makes me physically ill."

Charlotte remained silent through the tirade, her hand brushing along Abby's back.

Abby shuddered as the sobs eased the slightest bit. "This little girl had God knows what done to her by that maniac. What if we did something by removing her from the pod? It's one thing after another and I can't…it's like the walls are closing in."

A glass of water hovered in her peripheral vision. James' deep voice was surprisingly soft when he spoke, "Here. Drink this."

"James?" Abby took the glass. Though it shook in her grasp, she took several long swallows.

"Anne would blow my ass up if I just sat there and didn't help her mom." He crouched in front of her. "It sucks. All of it. We'll get through it, though. Always do."

"I hate to say it, but I agree with James." Charlotte helped James get Abby into a chair. She grabbed the plate of food and set it back in front of Abby. "We'll get through it. Annie will

36

wake up soon. They'll find Uncle Warren and figure out what's going on with him."

"I appreciate everything you've both done." Abby squeezed James' hand. "I'm so sorry for everything Warren has done and said to you. I can feel how much you and Annie love each other. I know you'll always protect her."

James cleared his throat, his gaze drifting away. He rubbed his free hand on the back of his neck. "She's the most important thing to me."

Abby leaned her elbows on the table in front of her. Her head pounded now with the weight of a thousand worries. She sank her head into her hands. "Promise me you'll take care of her."

"I swear to you I'll protect her with my life." James touched her back. "Try to eat. She'll kick all our asses if we don't eat."

A short laugh slipped free. The man had a point, and clearly knew her daughter. "You're right. I've never been good with the whole hurry up and wait game. I usually have Warren to help me. Now, I'm not even sure who my husband is anymore."

Charlotte slipped into the seat beside her. "All you need to do right now is focus on Annie and taking care of yourself. Don't worry about the rest. Take care of yourself and your daughter. Soon enough we will have to deal with everything else."

"You sound so much like your parents." Abby smiled over at Charlotte.

"I've been told it's usually a good thing to sound like them."

"Yes. It usually is."

Lucas walked into the nearly completed new mess hall. Talisa and Ethan leaned over a map spread out on one of the tables. "Ilana is not topside, but I do not believe she is in danger."

"Luke, man, none of the telepaths can find her. How is that not in danger? She disappeared into thin air. Again." The last word was a whisper, but Talisa's gaze snapped up to the young man. Ethan didn't seem to notice. His fingers linked behind his neck; tension radiating off him.

"Again?" Talisa stared at Ethan when he startled. "What does that mean?"

I—well—she—" Ethan flushed a bit, then groaned. "She didn't really disappear, but she was sort of phasing in and out like she was being transported to the *Enterprise*. It was back in our room and it only lasted a minute."

Lucas guessed there was much more to the story, the way Ethan avoided both of their eyes. He didn't pry, though.

Neither did Talisa. "Maybe a new power? It always takes her a minute to adjust."

38

"It doesn't seem like that." Lucas pondered for several minutes. He reached out in hopes the Spirits would give an answer, but as had been the case lately with Ilana, they were rather silent. "Apparently whatever message they have is meant for Ilana alone."

"What?" Talisa lifted her gaze to meet his.

"I have meditated on Ilana's troubles, and the Spirits have only told me that this is part of her journey. When I ask questions, they do not respond. I believe their message is meant for Ilana alone, when she is ready to listen. I do think they would tell me if Ilana was in danger." Lucas pursed his lips as his brother-in-law scoffed.

"Can you ask them to give back my wife then?" Ethan stopped his pacing, fists clenched at his sides.

"It does not work like that, unfortunately." Lucas sighed. "There is something that she is meant to learn."

"We'll get her back." Talisa set a hand on Ethan's arm. "Let's start from the beginning."

"She disappeared in Ravenhawk's meditation room." Lucas turned to head in that direction. "We were discussing searching for Warren, and she mentioned concern for Ethan."

"What about my dad? Did something else happen with him?" Ethan jogged behind them to catch up.

The corners of Talisa's mouth turned down in concern. "Let's find Ilana first. We'll talk about Warren later."

"For fuck's sake! Nothing is ever easy here, is it? Fine. First, we find my wife, and then someone tell me what the hell is going on with my father." Ethan punched a beam as they passed. "Jesus, does Danny know what's going on? Or Annie?"

"Ethan." Talisa stopped dead, turning to face him. "You grew up in this world. It's always a million crises at once. This time it happens to involve you personally, so it hits different. I get that, but you need to suck it up, buttercup. We can only handle one moment at a time."

The air itself condensed around them as Ethan glared at Talisa. Raindrops started to fall light as mist on Lucas' skin.

Tal pointed a finger in Ethan's face. "Don't you dare. You'll ruin the equipment, and I *will* make you stop. This telepathy may be new, but I'm a quick study and I know just what buttons to push to shut you down."

Ethan bristled a moment, then sagged. "I just want my wife back."

"Everything will work out as the Spirits intended, Ethan." Lucas touched his brother-in-law's shoulder. "Mother is right, we can only do one thing at a time. Right now, we will retrace our steps and find Ilana."

The trio moved through the halls to Chance's meditation room. Lucas pushed open the door so Talisa could enter ahead of him. "We met with the Chief in here. He was working with some herbs to create a tea."

"You and your sister joined him, and then what?" Talisa moved about the room seemingly at random. She stopped right in the spot where Ilana had disappeared, though he hadn't pointed it out. Her eyes closed and she took a deep breath.

"He briefed us on the situation. I took over the herbs for him. Ilana asked who knew and expressed concern for Ethan. Then, she was gone." Lucas paused at the mortar and pestle he'd been using.

"How does a human being just disappear? Are you sure she didn't just leave the room?" Ethan paced the length of the space.

"If she had just left the room, Lucas and I would still feel her presence." Talisa moved from the spot where Ilana had been to lean against the worktable.

"As I said, I do not feel as if she is in danger. I do not have any answers beyond that." Lucas grabbed more of the herbs he had been working with to toss into the mortar.

Ethan shouted at the ceiling, "Give me back my wife, damn it!"

"Yelling at the Spirits rarely results in the outcome you wish for." Lucas continued with his work.

"I just want her back." Tears welled in Ethan's eyes.

"We all do." Talisa turned to face Lucas. "What are you working on?"

"Attempting to recreate what I worked on earlier when she disappeared."

"Mom? Where did the Chief go?" Ilana's voice came from the exact spot she'd been standing when she disappeared.

"Babe!" Ethan wrapped his arms around her.

Ilana gasped at the ferocity of the hug, her arms all but pinned.

"Ilana." Lucas stepped toward his sister. None of this made sense, but she was back so now there was time to figure it all out. "What is the last thing you remember?"

"What do you mean, Lucas?" The words gasped out of Ilana. She wrapped her arms around her husband, and his grip seemed to loosen. She took a deep breath. "Chance was telling us about Warren. I blinked, and he's gone. Mom is standing in his place, and Ethan is hugging me so tight I might stop breathing."

Talisa reached out to touch her daughter's arm. "Baby, you've been missing for over an hour. You disappeared. From right where you're standing now."

"Disappeared? What are you talking about? I haven't moved from this spot." Ilana's gaze traveled between Lucas and her mother, wide-eyed in panic.

"You were standing there and then you were gone. We have not been able to locate you or speak with you." Concern ratcheted through Lucas.

"*Stop*," Ilana shrieked. "I haven't been missing. Ethan, let me go. You're suffocating me, literally. Please."

"Lana." Ethan released her but kept his hands on her shoulders. "Breathe, babe. It's okay. We were just worried."

Lucas backed off. Rather than face what was clearly a confused, and quite possibly terrified, Ilana, he grabbed some more herbs to add to the mortar. He resumed grinding. "We do not know what happened, but you were gone. Not here. The Spirits told me you were on a journey but did not expound on what happened."

"A journey?" Ilana's scoff carried through the words. "How is blinking and half the people in the room changing a journey?"

"Mother?" Lucas inclined his head toward the kettle. Talisa obliged with the fire needed to warm the water that Lucas had added to it by using his gift. He dropped the herbs into a tea ball, then into a mug.

"What is happening to me?" Ilana's voice cracked.

"Easy, baby." Talisa cupped Ilana's face in her hand. Her thumb brushed along her daughter's cheekbone. "We'll do our best to figure this out. Try to relax. You're back. That's all that's important right now."

Lucas handed Ilana the mug of tea. "Drink. It will help steady you. I do not know how, but we will help you find out what's happening."

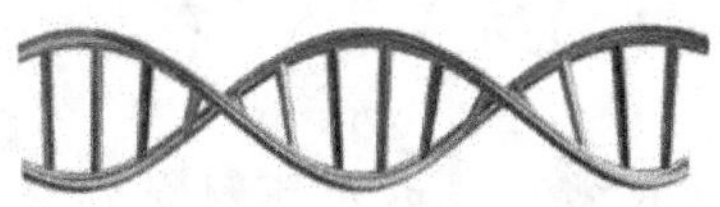

42

Warren clutched his laptop to his chest with one arm. With his other, he adjusted the bag of tools he'd slung over his shoulder. He had to find the answers that would tell him what the hell happened to him.

Abigail could have helped. He'd begged her for her help. She'd coldly refused him.

No wait. That wasn't right.

He never told her about the issues he'd encountered. He'd disconnected the comms link and told her to fuck off.

Enemy. She is one of them. Brainwashed. All of them. 01000101 01101110 01100101 01101101 01111001 00101110 00100000 01001011 01101001 01101100 01101100 00100000 01110100 01101000 01100101 01101101 00100000 01100001 01101100 01101100 00101110. Kill them. Send for 01010011 01110100 01100101 01100101 01101100 01100101.

"No. No. Not Gail. Never Gail. She loves me."

The dirt stairs spiraled down beneath him. The next expansion was dug nice and deep. Silent and dark, he could easily hide there. There were too many telepaths. He needed to find answers. He couldn't do that with so many searching for him, and for his brain.

He dug through the bag at his side for the flashlight. With it secure, and his way illuminated, he headed down the stairs. Down to the deepest corners of the expansions Chance had dug into the dirt and rock.

The moment he opened the laptop the screen filled with code. The zeros and ones flew by at an almost dizzying rate.

"Let's see what's going on here. Diagnostic process. Debug. Find virus."

Click. A mechanical tremor ran along his arm to his shoulder. That was new. And wrong.

Locate Anna Maria Johnson. Find program. Destroy.

"No! We need to bring her back. Save my daughter."

The laptop screen flipped from code to snow. The screen lit in streaks until a solid image formed. The picture began to move like in a movie. No, a memory.

"Who's ready for a night at the ball with their dear old dad?" Warren entered the room holding a velvet box.

"Daddy, we're going to be late." A young Annie nearly whined. No more than sixteen years old, she had a stern look on her face.

"I promise we'll make it, but I couldn't let you go without this." Warren placed a kiss on Annie's forehead. Before she could ask what it was, he turned to place a kiss on Abby's lips.

Annie smirked at her father. "You're late and bribing me with jewelry? Isn't there some lesson in here about what not to do with a guy?"

"She gets the smartass side from you, Gail. Open it, Annie. If you don't, we will be late." He chuckled at her pursed lips, and playfully stuck his tongue out at her.

The video froze in place, glitching across the screen. He touched a finger to the image of his daughter. Young, so young. Innocent. In an image that wasn't real. Hadn't ever happened.

After a few more glitches, the screen faded to snow again. Code stretched out across the snow until it ran steady and fast again.

"Annie," he whispered into the emptiness. "My baby."

A plant. Enemy. 01100101 01101110 01100101 01101101 01111001. Sent to destroy us. A weapon. Signal for help.

"Gods, no. She's not the enemy. She's my little girl." A tear slipped down his cheek.

She doesn't want you. Only wants him.

An image of James flashed on the screen before fading back to code.

44

It will destroy you. It already destroyed your marriage.

A growl grew deep in his chest, rumbling in his throat. The computer blurred in his eyes as rage poured through him. His fist shot into the earthen wall beside him, leaving a divot.

"They have destroyed *everything.* Steele turned Talisa and Roark, and they are turning everyone else one by one."

Realization of his words dripped through him like an icy cold bath. What was he saying? Warren shook his head to clear it. "No. They're my family."

They abandoned you. Talisa stole your wife and children. You must protect us. They need to be destroyed. Signal for help.

"Protect my family. I must protect my family." He pounded his human hand against his head to try to get rid of the insidious voice telling him these things. None of it made sense. What was happening to him? He dug through the bag of tools, extracting the screwdriver. A flick of his arm popped the hatch on the cybernetic arm. "Need to fix it. Help my family."

Fix yourself. Abandoned you. Wife picked them. Sons picked them. Daughter picked them. Toxic family. Eliminate them all.

"All of them need to die…no…wait. *Focus!*" His robotic arm swung back into the wall on the other side of him, this time leaving a sizable hole in the earth. A crackle ran through his body, echoing through his brain.

Ultimate weapon. Experiment thirteen. Unlucky in every way. The winner is out there. Find it. Destroy us all.

"No. No. *No.*"

Signal. A click and twitch jolted his arm. A sound like the old emergency warning system rang through his skull. *Signal for help. 01100101 01110010 01100001 01100100 01101001 01100011 01100001 01110100 01100101 00101110 00100000 01101011 01101001 01101100 01101100 00101110 00100000*

01100100 01100101 01110011 01110100 01110010 01101111 01111001 00101110. The disease needs to be eradicated.

"No. No. *Fuck.*" He gripped his hair tight with both hands. When he tried to pull his hands free, a wrench of pain went through his head. He looked down and saw that the robotic arm held a thick tuft of hair. Nothing made sense. What was wrong with him? "Gail. Help me. Please. I need you."

Gave up on you. Protect yourself. Protect us.

"Stop it." Warren glared at the mechanical arm. "My wife didn't give up on me. She was helping to bring Annie back."

That thing doesn't want you.

"Not a thing. She's real. She's, our daughter."

The screen shifted again. An image of Annie on the screen. Her voice rang through the dark cavern. "You scare me. I feel safer with James."

"I'll kill him." Another echo of the warning system through his brain. His shoulder twitched, his arm jerking. Another flash of anger coursed through him. "He stole my daughter."

Kill them. Send the signal. We can help. Take them all out. Save your traitorous wife for last.

"Gods, no. Not my family. Need to save my family." Images of Abby, Danny, and Ethan slid across the screen. A few mixed images from memories Annie had shared flashed through as well. He gripped the side of the laptop with his flesh and bone arm.

Why did his brain keep flipping like this? Save everyone, kill them. He was losing his mind. That was the only explanation. He needed to save his family by any means necessary.

Protect yourself. We will protect you. Send the signal.

46

"What signal?" He glared at his arm. "What do you want from me? I need to help them. Gail. Gail will help me."

Click. His cybernetic arm went for the screwdriver.

He managed to keep it away somehow. "What is wrong with you?"

Time short. Send signal. Elimination is the only way.

Warren blinked rapidly to clear his head. A jolt ran through his arm again. Several clicks followed it. "Make it stop! I need Gail."

Eliminate with the rest. Send the signal. Help will come.

"Who is this? What signal? I don't understand."

All will be made clear. Send the signal.

He threw his head back against the wall. Maybe if he kept doing it the screws loose in his head would go back into place. Nothing made sense anymore.

Maybe if he signaled for help it *would* fix everything.

Signal in progress…

"Ari. Get everyone to pull back." Joe's voice rang through Ariel's mind.

Ariel was in position in Warren's office. The wall of computer monitors spread before her. She adjusted her headset as she focused on the different images to get a better perspective on the situation. *"What's going on, Tiger? I can't see your position."*

"There's a bomb. They need to move back." Regret carried through his tone. A pit of concern settled like a stone in her belly.

"Everyone pull back! I repeat. Everyone pull back!" Ariel rushed through the screens to try to find Joe. To fully understand the situation.

"What gives, Red?" James' voice accompanied by the echo of gunfire carried through the communications.

"Get everyone out. Abort the mission. There's a bomb. That's an order, get out now!" She hit the keys at an almost frantic pace. She had to get a visual of Joe, and their friends.

48

"Pull back!" James' yells echoed through her head. Shouts passing between the others and more gunfire echoed through the headset.

Ariel tamped down the panic rising through her. It would do her no good to project such a thing to her husband. Once settled, she tapped into her connection with Joe again. *"Joe? Are you clear? James is pulling everyone back."*

No answer came right away. She could feel Joe's tension and concentration streaming back to her through the connection. He was focused. Dead focused.

She gulped against the lump in her throat. *"Tiger, talk to me."*

"I love you, Ariel."

Ariel startled awake. She inhaled sharply; her hand clutched her heart. The cold metal ceiling stared back at her, not caring about her inner turmoil. Tears slipped down along her features, dampening her hair. She no longer woke shrieking when the nightmares came.

They were not as lucky as Talisa and Roark. Joe didn't come back. He'd sacrificed himself so the others could live.

A year ago, she'd had a husband by her side, along with her daughters. Her family had been whole and complete. Despite the war they were in, she'd had hope.

It had taken her a month to recover from the sudden, brutal severing of the link she and Joe had shared.

Physically, at least, she had recovered.

Mental healing might never happen. She functioned as best she could so the girls wouldn't worry too much. Most days she spent in the unit she'd shared with her husband. Hell, his clothes still hung in the closet. She couldn't bear to part with them. Nor with the pictures that still lined the shelves.

"Joe," she whispered to the empty air. "I miss you."

She knew Joe was dead. It was a cruel fact she faced every minute of every day. Her soul still reached out to him as it always had. She could still feel the tattered remnants of their link at the edges of her awareness. Perhaps that was what kept her reaching for him mentally, even when she couldn't physically.

She pushed herself to sit on the edge of the bed. From under her shirt, she retrieved his dog tags. Her thumb trailed along the letters that spelled 'Maritime'.

"Goddess, I miss you. The kids suggested that if I talked to you, it would make me feel closer to you. It doesn't seem to help. I feel further away than I ever have." She swiped at the flow of tears streaming down her cheek.

"The others came back. All the Nashuk's. Talisa and Roark, they're back. They're back together. You weren't as lucky. *We* weren't as lucky. It's not fair." Ariel pressed a kiss to the dog tags. "Rest easy my love."

She'd managed to sit on the edge of the bed and sat there not motivated to do much else. Once upon a time she'd been an active and productive member of the resistance. Now she was little more than a burden to them.

"Mom?" Mackenzie's voice shattered her illusion of seclusion.

"In the bedroom, Kenzie." Ariel forced herself to her feet. To busy herself and not look like such a wreck, she tugged her hair into a messy bun. "Everything okay?"

"Just wanted to check on you." A sad smile marred her daughter's beautiful features. Evidence of how much she hadn't succeeded in not worrying her children. "I brought you some tea. Lucas created a new one for you."

"That was nice of him. He should save the resources, though. Unfortunately, there's no such thing as an endless supply any longer." Ariel was grateful for her daughters' visits. It kept her present, or at least as present as she allowed herself to be. "I'll put on some water."

"With Chance around, as far as herbs go, we sort of do." Mackenzie wrapped her arm around her mother. "Did you sleep okay?"

"As okay as I ever do." She patted her daughter's arm. "What about you and Lucas? You both doing well? I'm sure he's ecstatic that his parents are back."

Mackenzie's arm tightened around her. "He is happy to have them back. They've been dealing with the usual number of issues, but they plan to come see you soon."

"It's fine baby. I know there are more important things going on right now than checking on me. They are still in the fight." Ariel closed her eyes against the burgeoning tears. Mentally she reached for Joe as she always did. *"Joe, help me!"*

The mental call rushed along the tattered edges of their connection. Without her husband on the other end to receive it, it would dissipate into nothing. Like it always did.

But this time was different.

This time it rebounded back. The tiniest hint of the familiar brush of Joe's essence reflected back to her, clinging to those tattered edges, drawing them together the slightest bit. Shock weakened Ariel's knees until she crashed to the ground.

Mackenzie followed her. "Mom! Mom, what's wrong?"

A guttural sob ripped through her body. "Oh Goddess, Joe. Goddess, help me."

"Mom. Talk to me. What happened?" Mackenzie scrabbled around to face her.

"Joe!" Ariel screamed aloud as well as in her mind. Once again, another tingle of what felt like her husband.

"What happened?" Lucas' calm voice filtered through her panic. Had Mackenzie called him?

Ariel felt herself lifted on a pillow of water and carried to a nearby chair in the kitchen. Deep gasping breaths filled her lungs, but not enough. Panic closed off her lungs and throat. The whistle of the tea kettle made her jump. "Joe…"

"Ariel. Breathe." Lucas set a hand on her shoulder. "What occurred to cause this reaction?"

"I don't know." Panic or tears, maybe both, made her daughter's voice tremble. "We were talking about your parents coming to visit her, and she collapsed calling for my father."

"We knew their return would be difficult for her." Lucas moved around the kitchen, but she couldn't be bothered to pay attention to exactly what he was doing.

"Don't leave me. Come back, please. I can feel you. I know you're there somewhere. Joe, please." Ariel continued to reach for her husband, hardly able to believe what she knew was happening. Every time she called out another piece of him came back to her. No words, not yet, but him. Like he was reforming, which was impossible considering how he'd died. Still—before he'd died when they weren't openly communicating it had felt like this. An ever-present touch at the back of her mind.

Mackenzie set a mug in front of her. "Mom, drink this. It will help calm you."

Ariel shook her head so hard she thought she might shake it right off. The teas too often made her relaxed and she couldn't afford to sleep right now. She had to find Joe. "No. I don't want to go back to sleep."

"This will not make you sleep; I promise. It is only to calm you so you can tell us what happened." Lucas took the seat across from her.

52

"Please, Mom. We want to help." Mackenzie's hand rubbed along Ariel's back.

"Alright." With a shaky breath she brought the mug to her lips to take a sip. After just one sip, she set it back down.

"A little more Mom."

"I'd ask who the parent here is, but I haven't exactly been stellar in that department lately." Ariel gave her daughter a slight smirk before taking a few more sips. Despite her worry of falling asleep the tea did soften her frayed nerves. If there was one thing she could say about her son-in-law, he was a wizard with herbs.

"Sometimes we have to take care of our parents. Us, Nashuk's know that all too well." Lucas smiled warmly her way. "Better?"

"A little." She took her daughter's hand in her own.

"Can you tell us what happened?" Lucas set his hand on top of her and Kenzie's joined ones.

"I..." Ariel glanced between the two. "You're going to think I'm insane. I know it."

"Considering the world we live in; nothing is crazy."

"I felt Joe." Tears sprang forward again at the simultaneous gasp from the pair. "I told you it would sound insane. Search my mind, Lucas. You can see what happened. What I felt."

"With your permission." Lucas smiled sadly, then quietly entered her mind. Ariel could tell the second he connected Mackenzie as well. *"I see what you saw, what you felt. Will you try again for me?"*

"Joe..." Just as before the call stretched along the now-healing connection into the void. A small whisper of Joe returned to her awareness.

A strange voice echoed through the darkness. *"Hello?"*

Pain pulsed behind Annie's closed lids. She wondered if this was what a hangover felt like. A quick mental inventory led to the realization that not just her head, but her entire body hurt. Annie cracked her eyes open. The light blinded her, so she winced and shut them again.

"Easy Anne." James' concerned voice filtered into her confusion.

"James." Her throat was rough like sand lined every inch of it. The word had been more of a croak really, than her usual voice. Her mother. Where was her mother? She had to keep her mother away from Warren. If he had tried to kill her, what would he do to her mother and brothers? Uselessly she tried to move her arms and legs, but they wouldn't respond to her wish to sit.

A glass broke near her, a female gasp following behind. It pulled her attention from the man with her. Had it been her mother? Talisa?

"Don't force it, Annie." Roark's face entered her peripheral vision as she opened her eyes again. His fingertips glided along her wrist, then her throat. A pen light flashed in each eye, garnering another wince. "Your body is taking it's time rebooting, so to speak. We're going to sit you up in the bed, okay?"

All Annie could muster was a curt nod, closing her eyes again. James' hands slipped behind her back to lift her to sit. Each metal clank of the notches on the bed reverberated through her body despite his assistance. Only once she'd been situated in a sitting position did she attempt to open her eyes again. The three sets of concerned eyes that peered back made her question just how long she'd been unconscious.

Talisa's concern was the first to disappear. She offered Annie a bright smile. "How are you feeling, Annie?"

"Sore, mostly. It's weird. I can feel the computers again, but I don't have the same control I did when I was trapped inside. Not sure about how my other gift is faring, though." Annie laced her fingers with James. The need for direct contact seemed to burn deep inside her.

"I'd say it still works. You broke a beaker when you were trying to wake. I've never seen a liquid boil and freeze at the same time in the same space." Abby beamed at her daughter. "It's good to see you awake."

"It's good to be awake."

James pressed his lips to her temple. "Can you tell us what happened? You were terrified when we pulled you out of the pod."

A shudder ran through Annie at the memory. "Water?" She took the cup Roark offered, taking several long sips from the straw.

"Annie?" A wave of calm accompanied her mother's question.

"Thanks, Mom." She set the cup down and squeezed Abby's hand. Her eyes fluttered shut as she inhaled a deep, cleansing breath. There was no way to sugar coat it.

Talisa looked up from her notes. Her head tilted as she nodded to Annie. "Take your time. We aren't going anywhere."

"I told James I loved him, and I jumped into the pathways back to my body." James' grip tightened on her hand. She ran her thumb along the back of his hand to calm him. "Everything was normal, just like when I jumped into the computer to begin with. Until it wasn't."

"What do you mean?" Abby sat on the foot of the bed next to Annie's legs. Her hand rested on Annie's calf like she needed the contact as much as Annie did.

"At first it looked like a bit of errant code. I thought maybe it was pieces of—well—me. The parts that had degraded in the laptop, then followed me. Then it started to take form. It started saying one thing on repeat. The voice was as distorted as the code at first, but it started to take form like I had." Despite her attempts to be strong, tears escaped her control to slip down her face.

"We're here, Anne. It's okay." James ran his fingers along her scalp. The soothing sensations coursed down her spine.

"What was it saying?" Abby continued to squeeze Annie's calf. Waves of calm continued to flow through the room.

"Locate Anna Maria Johnson. Find program. Destroy." Annie offered a tremulous smile she didn't feel. Her hand shook as she gripped James' hand. "It took a human form and voice. Warren's."

"Are—" Abby cleared her throat. "Are you sure?"

"I'm so sorry, Mom."

"Don't you apologize. This isn't your fault. We'll deal with it, somehow." Abby took a shaky breath. "I wouldn't ever let him hurt you. I only wanted to make sure."

"I'm positive. It was his coding. His style of writing a virus." She gasped, sitting up straighter. The pain wrenched through her body at the movement. "Oh no. Is the pod connected to the network?"

Talisa squeezed her foot. "No. We never connected it to the main network. It's only connected to the tablets that were attached to it."

56

"The virus could eventually break through the safety measures I put in place when I was trying to escape. It's contaminated the pod for sure, but I would recommend a full network sweep for any other possible iterations or variations of the virus."

"Right now, you need to rest and let your body figure out how to let you be in the driver seat." Roark refilled her water and added another bag of saline to her pole. "In a few hours we'll see how you do with walking and standing. Are you hungry? We can get you some broth from the kitchen."

Annie huffed out a breath. "How long am I going to be trapped here?"

Roark chuckled, giving her shoulder a squeeze. "Probably not as long as you might think. We are taking it slow to see how your body adjusts. If you can keep down the broth and some tea, we'll move onto solid foods. With your new healing ability, I don't think it'll be long before you're running circles around James."

Annie's gaze flipped between James and his father. "What healing? I don't have a healing ability. I'm not animal."

"Actually." Talisa grinned from the foot of the bed. "In order to keep your DNA from degrading again we had to isolate a portion of James' for the healing. It keeps everything where it should be."

"Ma?" James half rose, staring at his mother with wide eyes. Clearly, he hadn't known it either. "What will that do to her?"

"Keep her alive. She'll change and grow like any of us. The healing is likely to be slower than ours due to the small amount of healing, and it not being tied to an animalistic gene." Talisa slipped an arm around her husband, then nodded at them.

"But it is there and will help you heal faster than you would otherwise."

Abby launched herself across the bed to envelop Talisa in a hug. "Thank you."

Talisa returned the hug with a smile. "No need for thanks. We're just glad it worked. For now, we'll see about getting you some food. After you eat, we'll work on getting you mobile."

"Seriously…all of you, thank you." Annie squeezed James' hand tightly, then loosened her hold slightly. "I can't tell you what it means to me that I'm here. Alive."

"It means just as much to us. Welcome to the family, Annie."

"Don't leave me. Come back, please. God, please come back. I can feel you."

Pain and anguish in the strangers' voice ripped through Kaliya like a palpable force. She almost recoiled in reaction to it. Though able to keep her physical reaction in check, her heart constricted in her chest. Whoever was behind the voice seemed to be in so much pain. No, she knew they were in pain. It echoed through her like a shadow behind her own emotions.

Taylor's voice reverberated through the tank from outside it as she gave orders to the technicians in the room. Her tone carried frustration, but the oddly needling voice of the General had gone away. Hopefully that meant he had left.

Kaliya remained still and quiet, not wishing to be poked and prodded again. Her body relaxed as though in sleep.

A small tap on the glass preceded Taylor's voice again. "I know you aren't asleep yet, Kaliya. It's safe to open your eyes."

Kaliya allowed one eye to open to peek out into the room. "Is something wrong, ma'am?"

Taylor folded her arms across her chest. One hip stuck out as she smirked. "I could ask you the same thing."

"I'm a little sore from training today. Nothing a good night's sleep won't cure. I do heal well enough." Normally something like the voice she'd heard was something she'd tell Taylor immediately. For some reason instinct told her to remain silent. This was something to be kept quiet. To herself. Private. Even if privacy seemed pointless when you were on display in a tank most of the time.

"Are you sure? You know you can trust me."

Kaliya wanted to, but how much could you trust the person performing the experiments? Even if she was under orders, it was still her hands doing the dirty work. No, she'd trusted Taylor before. Before she could spill her confusion, Kaliya thought it better to change the subject. "The general sounded angry."

"One of our compounds was attacked by the Infected." Taylor grimaced, then somehow managed to smile. The smile seemed forced; it didn't reach her eyes. "There were losses."

"I'm sure the General will create a plan that will return the favor soon."

"Without a doubt." Taylor tapped a few keys on the outside of the tank. "Get some sleep. Tomorrow is going to be a long day. I'm sure there will be extra training involved."

"I will see you in the morning." Kaliya prayed the woman would leave the room quickly. She had to process what was happening to her.

Something strange inside her wanted her to reach out to the strange voice. Though she'd never heard it before, it was familiar. It soothed something in her soul that had felt—broken. No, not broken. Separated. Apart from the rest. It had happened months ago when they'd first made it so she could breathe underwater.

60

At the same time, she'd begun to be able to sense the tiniest of vibrations in the air, which was enhanced when they first put her in the tank to test that her ability to form gills had taken hold. The procedure that had added these abilities had also left that sense of everything being off. She'd often had that feeling after they'd changed her, but usually it faded.

This time it had hung around.

The door to the lab slid open, and the lab emptied. The lights in the room flickered off, leaving only the lights around the bottom of her tank on. She closed her eyes, letting the peace of solitude wash over her.

"Joe…"

"Hello?" A wave of surprise carried back to her, causing her to open her eyes. Had she lost her mind? Perhaps she *should* have brought this oddness up to Taylor. What if there was something wrong with the modifications they'd made?

"I can feel you, Joe. Please come home." Anguish colored the voice until it cracked even though it was not spoken aloud.

"How are you able to talk to me?" She didn't want to scare the woman off, but she was curious about what was happening. Something in her also wanted to help. Answers were important, but she wanted to comfort whoever this was. In a way she'd never seen comfort herself. *"I was given much, but I'm not telepathic."*

"You know how. Don't you remember? Our connection. Our link. We've been able to talk to each other this way for so long, I can hardly remember a time we couldn't. Where are you? We'll come get you." A hope now lifted the voice.

Hope Kaliya couldn't allow herself to feel. She was a tool. A weapon to be used against others like this woman. She knew she should end whatever this was but couldn't help herself. *"What is your name?"*

"Oh God. What have they done to you? Why don't you remember? It's Ariel. Your wife." Images of a red-haired women and two young women filtered through the connection. *"The mother of your two beautiful daughters."*

Kaliya's heart constricted in her chest. She rushed forward as if the woman stood before her. Hands planted against the side of the tank, she stared into the dark room. No. It had to be a trick. How could she not tell it wasn't a man speaking?

"Joe?"

"Listen to my voice. I'm not Joe. I don't know why you believe otherwise."

"I can feel my husband. I can." The connection flickered like static, a sob coming through clear as day. *"You are my husband. I know you are. I feel you. I'm not crazy."*

"My name is Kaliya. I do not believe you are crazy, but I am not your husband."

"You are an Exceptional!"

"I am one of the Infected, but I'm different."

Anger pulsed back. *"Do not call yourself Infected."*

"General Steele has been generous and given me many gifts. The gifts of others have been grafted onto me. He infected me with more so that others would not have to suffer."

"What?!" Shock slammed back through the link hard enough to make Kaliya rush backward from the force. Quick as it had started, the sensation disappeared. The faintest whisper lingered in the back of her mind that it remained but had been blocked from the other side.

"Ariel? Are you there? Can you hear me?"

Only silence came back. What had happened to her? Where had she gone?

Kaliya hoped she was well.

Moreover, she hoped she would return.

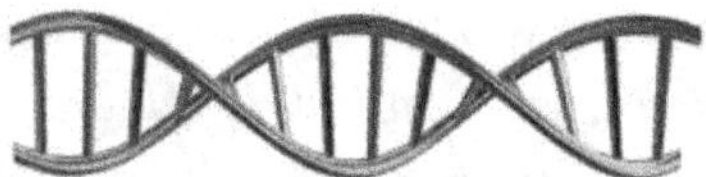

Talisa stretched out with her mind as wide as she could. So many voices echoed back throughout the compound. Families enjoying meals together, children playing games, couples, individuals, so many people they were supposed to be protecting through the endless chaos.

She quickly dismissed so many as not the one she was looking for. When she tried to find Warren specifically, white noise was all she found. Like a television that no matter what channel you tried, just showed you the annoying snow.

The image brought back memories of life on the reservation when they were young. She'd get so frustrated over the lack of cable TV when her parents insisted on living as much in the past as possible. The frustration of her youth enhanced her current frustration until she released a low growl. "Damn it."

"Easy, Kajah." Chance massaged her shoulders.

"It's just like when my parents refused to get cable."

"What?" He laughed low. "That's a random reference."

"Not as random as you might think." She blew out an annoyed breath. "He presents as static and snow much like our television did with those damned useless rabbit ears."

This time Chance laughed outright. "My parents got cable before yours did. Made you so mad because I didn't want to watch TV, I wanted to play outside."

"Of course, it annoyed me. I wanted to watch Bill Nye."

"Your father always said—"

"Nature gives us everything we need." She clasped her hands with his when tears sparked in her eyes. "If only that were still true. We could live so well up there on the surface."

"We will. One day."

"You sound so sure." She rubbed her hands over her face. "Ugh. What am I doing? I need to stop reminiscing, stop dreaming. I need to find Warren."

"You won't find him when you're this tense."

"Watch me." She closed her eyes. Once again reaching out across the compound, even up to the surface. Still nothing came back but snow and static. She groaned, pinching the bridge of her nose. "That computer brain of his is infuriating when it's being used against you."

"Can I say it?"

"Don't you dare, smartass."

"Lucas has had his telepathy much longer than you have, and he's having trouble getting a bead on him, too. Ethan and Ilana are with him now, on their way to his and Abby's unit."

"Your ability to remain calm is so annoying sometimes, Sani."

"And yet, you still love me." He gave her a quick hug. "Now, close your eyes. Take a deep breath."

"Meditation isn't going to help right now."

"How do you know? Have you even tried? Stop being a brat. Close your eyes."

She blew out a whoosh of breath. "Fine. I'll try it, but we have to find him soon."

"And we will. I have every confidence in that. We aren't going to enjoy this part of the journey, but it will get us to where we need to be." Chance took her hands in his own. "Don't make me tell you again."

"You do and I might punch you."

64

"Then do it."

Talisa screwed her eyes shut. She popped one open to peek at him. The look of frustration creasing his features made her grin. "Oh, how I've missed you, C."

He dropped a kiss on her forehead. "I've missed you, too. Quit stalling."

After she'd stuck her tongue out at him, she did as she'd been told, for real. She rolled her neck from side-to-side to remove the tension. Then she took a deep, cleansing breath. Chance's mind, so close to her, stood out. A quick switch of focus took her to the lab where Roark, Abby, Annie, and James remained.

"That's it, T. Focus. Filter out what you don't need." Chance's calm voice filtered into her brain so easily, he'd always been welcome as her best friend. He got in nearly as easily as Roark.

"Don't be so smug. I still haven't found him. Wait..."

In a weird burst, the static she'd been hitting every time splintered apart. Warren's voice hit her in a burst. *"Not Gail. Never Gail. She loves me."*

"I've got something." Right as she focused on the voice, it flickered out into snow again. She'd been so close. "Damn it."

"Take another deep breath. Let it flow. Try not to force it." Soothing as a warm fire, Chance's voice poured over her. His thumb ran in slow circles over the top of her hand reminding her of their physical connection and his support.

"Easy for you to say," Tal mumbled.

Chance snorted; the soothing tones dropped from his voice quickly. "Yes, smartass. It is easy for me to say. Helps that I've seen you do amazing things before."

"Sani," she teased. A smile rose despite her frustrations. "I'm married, remember? We can't talk about such naughtiness any longer."

"Anyway." He cleared his throat, squeezing her hands. "Enough. Time for round two."

"Chicken."

He tapped the back of her hand. "Kajah."

"Right. Round two. Like a fight. Prize fight, or chicken?"

His lip twitched like he might join in her sudden laughter. "Talisa."

"Sorry. I'm sorry." She did her best to gather herself. "I don't know why that tickled me."

"Because you're nervous, and you're worried about what we're going to find."

"Know it all." Talisa blew out a slow, cleansing breath. "Focus."

Tal did as instructed this time. Once again she started in the area they were in. One by one she pushed aside any thoughts that weren't from the mind she searched for. For a moment she lingered on Ariel and Kenzie, drawn by the note of panic in the women. One fiasco at a time, though. They'd have to revisit that later.

"Gods, no. She's my little girl." In another burst of static, Warren's voice crept forward.

"Warren?" The harder she pushed, the more the resistance of snow hit her.

"Kajah?" Chance's thoughts brushed against hers. *"You look confused."*

"I can't get through this damned static." She growled deep in her chest. Fists clenched; she wanted nothing more than to punch something—but as only Chance was in front of her, she held the instinct back.

66

"Ask Annie for help."

Talisa's eyes popped open. She quirked a brow at him in frustration. "Annie's only been in her body for a few hours. She's exhausted. How, exactly, is she supposed to help with this?"

"Do what you did when you focused on Warren. Ask her to let you in, and then shut down her brain the way Warren has. Maybe it'll give you a better idea of what to look for."

"That's…actually not a bad idea."

"Thank you for your support."

"Okay." She shook out the tension that had reappeared when Warren blocked her again. Instinctively she held out her hands to let Chance take them again. She closed her eyes, counting her breaths in a pattern of three.

Chance's thumbs continued their rhythmic pattern along the back of her hands. The soothing motion allowed her to relax fully again.

Talisa took her attention back to the lab. The familiar presence of Roark in her mind drew her there easily. Not wanting to startle Annie, she approached her mind quietly. *"Annie?"*

"Talisa? Is everything okay?" Annie seemed even more relaxed than Tal in her current state. If it weren't for the hint of the underlying desire to get out of bed, she'd be totally calm.

"Could you help me? It's a simple task that won't require use of your body at all."

"Are you using me for my mind, then?"

"You could say that." Talisa laughed in her mind. *"You and Warren can turn your brain off from a telepath. Hide behind a sort of static. If you could, would you try to do that for a minute so I can see what it feels like?"*

"Sounds easy enough."

"You'd think. But wait." Talisa touched on her son's mind, bringing him in on the mental conversation. Soon as she'd updated, she added, *"I'll need you to relay between us when she's blocking me."*

"Got it, Mom." James' also seemed the most relaxed she'd ever known him to be.

Not wanting to dwell on that just yet, she focused more on Annie, though keeping James in the loop. *"Annie, I'd like you to slowly put the block in place."*

Annie's brain remained open at first. Little by little static crept across her thoughts, hindering their connection. Spirals of ones and zeros funneled to a central point. They fanned out in layers to form a sort of wall between them.

"Good. Now, James. Ask her to bring it down, and then do it again a little faster."

The three of them repeated the exercise several times until Talisa had a good feel for what she was looking at. *"Thank you both. Get some rest. We'll try and get you out of bed when I get back down there."*

"Thanks, Mom."

"Thanks, Talisa."

The second she opened her eyes; Chance smiled her way. "Did it help?"

"Actually, it did. Funny how you do sometimes have good ideas."

He chuckled softly, moving to the stove to pour hot water into mugs. "I know it's surprising. I'm only the chief of our tribe. You've always been the smart one, anyway."

"Oh, only in some ways."

He held one of the steaming mugs to her. "Drink this."

"Am I going to get smaller?"

"We are far from Wonderland, Kajah."

7

"Well, is it ready?" Steele's voice rumbled into Taylor's lab.

Taylor kept her back to the man so she might safely roll her eyes at him. His lack of decorum might have been pushed off as military, but she thought it was more. The man was single minded when it came to the Infected. She tried to make her response pleasant. "Hello to you too, General."

"I don't have time for your attempts at being witty today." The General slammed a stack of folders on her desk.

Taylor took a bracing breath. She glanced at the creature floating in the tank seemingly oblivious to what happened in the lab. With a forced smile, she turned to face the man. "Yes. I believe Kaliya can handle anything you throw at her. She managed today's training rather well. I can't say the same for the soldiers she trained against. They lack the ability for improvisation."

"My soldiers are fine. Trained to the hilt." He huffed at her attack on his soldiers. "They're learning to fight against those blasted Infected. We lost too much research with the flooding of our other facility."

"All those poor souls lost—"

Steele cut her off, "They were soldiers. They knew what they signed up for. What's tragic is the research we lost. Those pods. All of the breakthroughs Talisa made."

"We'll recreate her research. We've apprehended more Exceptionals." Taylor bristled against his adoration for Talisa's research. The woman was brilliant, certainly, but so was Taylor. She retrieved a file from her cabinet. "Great progress has been made."

Steele laughed, but his look was hard as his name indicated. "Great progress? We lost everything Talisa did for us, even if she doesn't remember doing it. She's the sharpest mind we've ever found. How long will it take for you to get to her level? Forever."

Taylor gritted her teeth against the insult. It would be deadly to argue with him. She never bothered, even if it was sorely tempting. Talisa, Talisa, Talisa. She swore the man forgot his hatred of the Exceptionals when it came to her. Obsession, pure and simple. "I'll need more Exceptionals to work with in order to make any progress."

"Your main priority now is ensuring *it* is ready to go against the Infected on our next attack." Steele's grin turned sinister. He rubbed his hands together like some old-school villain. "I have a feeling we'll have the location of the main resistance base soon."

"Oh? I didn't realize we were closer to finding them." She sat down and hit a few keys to bring up Kaliya's latest statistics. "Kaliya's strength and endurance are triple that of a regular human. As you already know she can breathe underwater and see further than any of us. She regenerates as well as controls water. I'd say she is damn near perfect."

"It. Not she. Not whatever god-forsaken name you chose. I keep having to tell you this. It is not a person. It has the DNA of male and female Infected grafted onto it. *It* is an abomination. A tool. Don't try to humanize it."

"I've found you get better results with a little honey instead of the vinegar that runs through your veins. The subjects react better." God, how she'd come to loathe the man. It wasn't that she liked Exceptionals, or Infected, or whatever you wanted to call them. She'd come on board to help with some research. It was a good way to further her own agenda. Conversations like this one made her want to unleash all the test subjects on him and stand back to watch.

"I don't care how you get results, so long as you get them. This is all taking so long. Talisa would have this all solved in half the time it took you to name this thing."

"Well, Talisa isn't here, is she? She's Infected. She isn't coming back, and she hates you, which means you're stuck with those of us that are willing to help you with your cause." Taylor turned to glare at the man. What was the worst he could do to her? Kill her? He'd be back to square one. Again. This late in the game, he couldn't risk it.

"Watch your tone, Taylor. You *are* replaceable. Don't you remember what happened to Tara?" Steele's lips curved into a malicious smirk.

"I remember." Taylor turned back to her screen to hide her reaction. Tara—her twin. Steele had a theory that one of them was okay, but two of them would be better, more efficient. She'd been killed by Exceptionals. Steele attempted clones with disastrous results. Lord only knew if he had attempted any other clones after Talisa escaped. None of those created in Talisa's absence had survived more than a few weeks. Even those of experiment thirteen had only lasted a few months at best.

"Good. You're getting a little too big for your britches. Remember your place. You're only here because I allow it. Now make sure that thing is ready to go soon. We will have the location in our hands sooner rather than later, and it needs to be ready to attack with the rest of the soldiers. The Infected won't know what hit them."

"Yes sir. Taylor would play his game, but she refused to call Kaliya 'it'.

"Electricity might be nice. We just captured one with that ability. Cut it up if you must in order to give the weapon more power. Maybe even invisibility." Steel made his demands like he was ordering from a restaurant menu. Taylor bit her tongue against the urge to ask if he wanted fries with that.

"I'll see what I can do. The process takes time and Kaliya will need time to recover after a procedure. She might not be ready in time if you think we'll have the location soon." It wasn't a lie; the process did take time. However, the last thing Taylor wanted to do was inflict more pain on Kaliya. The woman had already endured so many procedures she barely looked human anymore.

"Fine." Steele spoke through gritted teeth. "Make sure it's ready to deploy soon. It's better to save the resources. When we're successful it will have to be destroyed anyway. Can't have any lingering Infected around once we wipe out the rest."

Panic gripped Taylor's chest. Destroy Kaliya? She was a masterpiece, perfect. Taylor had put so much of herself into this project. "Sir. I would suggest delaying that."

"Do you think you know better than me?"

"Of course not, sir. I'm only suggesting a delay. Even if we eradicate the Infected in the U.S. there are still plenty in the rest of the world. It doesn't stop the infection, it keeps spreading. All we'll have done is slow the problem." As much as it turned her stomach, Taylor knew she had to play to his ego. "You could use Kaliya to save the world."

"Hmmm. You have a point. Home is just the beginning. This must be eradicated worldwide. Continue, then. Make sure it is ready."

"I will, sir." Taylor blew out a breath she hadn't realized she was holding when he left the room. She needed an escape plan. Steele became more unhinged by the day.

She lifted her gaze to Kaliya. They could escape together in the chaos of the battle. It was dangerous to even think of putting her trust in one of them.

But what choice did she have?

Abigail gripped the chair in front of her for something solid to hold onto. Chance leaned against the desk. Talisa and Roark stood near him. The meeting felt so surreal. Granted, she'd just left the room where her daughter had been brought back to life after transferring her consciousness into a computer. Nothing should feel surreal anymore.

And yet...

"Abby?" Chance prompted gently.

"I'm sorry." Abby shook her head to push aside the distracting thoughts. "What?"

"I asked how you felt about how we were handling the situation."

"What is there to say? My husband tried to kill our daughter before she could be returned to us. He's already attacked Elan and James." Abigail's shoulders dropped. She stared at the floor. The man she'd loved, married, had children with. He was a monster. "There really isn't any question. Is there?"

"Abs, just because it might be the right decision, doesn't make it an easy one." Roark's tone and expression was as if he waited for the inevitable explosion.

"Roark is right." Talisa stepped closer. The sympathetic expression she wore bordered on pity, though she felt none from her friend. It made Abby's heart swell at the flow of love she felt from her friends. "You've been so focused on Annie that you haven't had much time to process.

"Process? Process that the man I loved tried to kill our daughter and two of your children. Being around him and his rage makes me physically ill to the point that you needed to put a block in my mind in order to keep me from acting like a raging bitch." Tremors seemed to radiate from her core. Abby gripped the seat even tighter to prevent them from escaping.

Chance crossed his ankles, his gaze still intent on Abby. "All of that might be true, but none of it is your fault."

"I know that, damn it," Abby snapped at him. "What do you want to hear? That I agree with tossing him in a containment unit, even separating him from his gift? That he needs to be *taken care of*? How about we add in the fact he built the network that keeps this place running. He could cripple us at any minute. For better or worse. Those were our vows. It doesn't matter if it's right, it all still feels like I've abandoned my husband."

"Easy." Tal took another step closer.

"Don't *easy* me, Tal. Do you have any idea how tired I am? Tired of being the one everyone expects to be sensible. Tired of keeping everyone else calm, making sure everyone else is happy. It didn't bother me before—I had my family." Her fists clenched at her sides, the emotions creeping up along her, no matter how much love Tal shoved in her direction. "Now that family is fractured."

"I understand."

"*No*. You don't." Tremors ran through her body. Tears tracked down her cheeks. "When am I allowed to fall apart? When am I allowed to grieve my husband going bat-shit crazy? My marriage imploding? My daughter *dying* and coming back to life?"

"Abigail." Chance moved closer.

"No. I can't. I can't do this. I can't keep it together for everyone else. I can't bolster the hope of the entire resistance anymore. I can't. *I can't. I can't.*" The second Chance got close enough; she started beating his chest with her fists in emphasis.

Talisa moved fast and surrounded Abby from the opposite side until both her and Chance had their arms around Abby. "Then don't. Let it out. We've got you."

"Oh God! What am I going to do? He's gone. My husband is gone. I can't save him. I need to protect the kids." Her knees gave out and Talisa and Chance's arms tightened around her to the point of crushing her as they guided her to the floor.

Chance pressed a kiss to her forehead. "Abby, throughout everything you have been there for all of us. That doesn't mean you can't take time for yourself to fall apart occasionally. We're here for you too."

"How? How do we do that Chance? In the middle of a war? What happens when I stop boosting everyone?" The tears continued to run tracks down her cheeks and dripping onto Chance's shirt.

"People adapt. Everyone in this place is trying to survive. We all do it the best we can." Talisa smoothed down Abigail's hair.

"We're all fucked in the head after everything Abs. Some more than others." Roark's voice startled her. She'd almost forgotten he was there midst her breakdown.

"Warren seems the worst off. I don't understand what's happening to him. This is not the man I feel in love with." A choked sob escaped against Chance's chest.

Roark knelt next to the group on the floor. "You have to know we're here for him too. We gotta find him and deal with the issue so we can help him. Afterwards, you can punch him for making you sick."

A short and sniffly laugh emerged between the pair holding her. "Sorry Chance. I got your shirt all wet."

"It's fine, Abby." Chance stroked her hair. "We lost a lot in all of this, but soap and water weren't one of the things we lost. We are here for anything you need. Even when it feels like a million things are going on at once."

"I've been so preoccupied with Annie and Warren. What the hell did I miss?" Abigail pushed up on her legs in an effort to stand. Chance and Talisa helped her.

"You know, the usual. Ariel was freaking out to the point that Kenzie had Charlotte sedate her and Ilana blinked out of existence for over an hour." Talisa loosened her grip on Abigail.

"What the hell? Is Ilana okay? Is Ethan with her? Wait, why is Ariel freaking out? We knew you guys coming back would make her melancholy, but freaking out?" She didn't release her grip on Chance's arms.

"Didn't you just have a breakdown about not being able to take on anymore?" Roark smirked at her.

"Okay, smartass. I had a freak out but I'm not going to let people suffer." The smirk on her face mirrored his.

Talisa chuckled behind her. "You never could deal with one thing at once Abby."

"Who can with this group?" Abigail rubbed the back of her hand along her cheeks to erase the tracks from her tears.

"Fair." Chance smiled down at her. "Is there anything we can do to help?"

"Find my husband and help me figure out what's wrong with him so we can fix him."

"We're working on it. Lucas and Ilana are getting ready to search the lower level now." Talisa squeezed Abigail's hand. "Don't bury it anymore, Abby. We're all in this together."

"Well, that's not a happy face." Inessa pulled Chance's office door shut behind her.

A smile tugged at the corners of Chance's mouth. He motioned for her to come towards him with one finger. "It wasn't, but seeing you makes it better."

"I can see that. The red and grey are draining from your aura. What's going on there, Chief?" Inessa laid her hands on his chest.

"Talisa and Roark just left with Abby. We're still trying to find Warren." He wrapped his arms loosely around her waist. "What have you been up to?"

"Same. Charlotte and I were trying to follow the threads. Best we can tell is he is down a level." Her face grew solemn. "Whatever is going on with him, his connections are withering. They pulse for the briefest moment and then fade again. Something is seriously wrong with him."

"We know. I can only hope that once we find him there is a way to help him. Abby is struggling. Hell, we all are." Chance tightened his arms pulling her closer. "Thank you for helping. How is it going with Charlotte?"

Inessa hesitated, "I'd say better. She's a remarkable young woman. Me being a mother, even if just from a DNA perspective, still feels insane to me."

"The DNA tests came back?" He ran his fingers along her spine.

"They did. We're taking it slow. How did you accept it so easily?"

"By the time she and Elan had been kidnapped we were already in the middle of the insanity with Steele and trying to survive. It wasn't long after that she was born. Tal and Roark ran tests when we got her back, and it was there in black and white. I wasn't going to deny her. Not to say there weren't growing pains between me and Roark."

"You never thought they were crazy?" Inessa's forehead wrinkled in concern.

"They had both already worked for Steele with Abby and Warren. We all knew how crazy he was. After we got her back, I held her, and I felt a connection to her. It doesn't matter to me she isn't my daughter in the traditional sense. I love her." Chance shifted to search her eyes. "No one expects you to accept it like we did."

"I know. I see the thread forming. I'm not sure what's weirder. That I instantly have a daughter or that I'm already hooking up with one of her fathers."

Chance chuckled, "Well, it would be weird if you were hooking up with both of her fathers."

Inessa smirked up at him, "Alright, smart ass."

"Sorry." He leaned down and brushed his lips across hers. "Are we just hooking up?"

"I…" She pursed her lips and studied his face for a moment. "Incoming, Chief."

"Incoming?"

The vision hit him out of nowhere. Warren gripped his hair with one hand. Tears streamed down his face. A video of him giving a jewelry box to a younger version of Annie played on his laptop in front of him. Snow replaced the image of Annie smirking at her father.

"Gods no, she's my little girl." Tears slipped down Warren's cheek.

The snow formed into an image of James. A growl filled the cavern Warren sat in. His fist shot out leaving a divot in the wall behind him.

Chance winced as the vision faded. He took a deep breath in and blew it out slowly. "Fuck, that hurt."

"You're still tensing when they come on Chance. I could see it starting in your aura right before it started. What did you see?" Inessa ran her fingers through his hair.

"Warren. You're right, he's down below. Hard to see exactly where he is. It's dark and we've started on a few sections to build our way down." He closed his eyes and took a few more deep breaths to center himself.

"Well, they are on the right track then. How are you feeling about locking him up?"

"Not something I want to do, but it's necessary. It's the only way we can attempt to help him. If we don't someone is going to get hurt." Chance tightened his lips; his eyes open again.

"You want to help him that's the important part. This is your family and part of your family is hurting. Even if you can't explain it." Inessa smiled up at him and cupped his cheek in her hand. "I have faith you will figure it out."

"Got me figured out already?"

"For the most part." She winked at him.

80

He snaked his arm around her waist pulling her tight against him. "Most part, huh? So back to my question before the powers that be decided to change the channel on me. What are we doing, Nessa?"

"Right now? We're standing in your office talking. Was there something else you'd rather be doing?" Inessa wrapped her arms around his neck with a wry smile.

"When you look at me like that, there is definitely something else I'd rather be doing. Too much is going on now though. *Are* we just hooking up?" Chance felt the heat rise in his face as he asked.

"I'm not sure how to answer that. We haven't known each other that long. We're in the middle of a war. Can I say I don't know without you overthinking it?" Her fingers danced along the back of his neck.

"What makes you think I'm going to overthink it?"

"I can see how skeptical you are. Grey just crept back into your aura."

Chance chuckled with a shake of his head. "You have an unfair advantage on me there."

"We don't know what tomorrow is going to bring. Hell, in the short amount of time we've known each other we found out we share a kid…with another couple. I haven't run yet."

"I'll have to work harder on giving you a reason to stay then."

"I'm not sure you'll have to work too hard on that, but like you said, there's too much going on right now."

Knuckles rapped on the door before it opened, and Charlotte entered. "Popsicle, we've got a problem."

A groan rumbled through Chance's chest. He dropped his head back to stare at the ceiling. "New or old?"

Charlotte chewed on her a bottom lip. "New facet to a really old problem."

"That doesn't bode well." He loosened his grip on Inessa. "What is it?"

"I think I need to borrow Nessa."

"Your mom mentioned that she had to be sedated. Is this from Tal and Roark coming back?" Chance pursed his lips. Ariel had nearly been mentally destroyed when Joe died. The woman deserved some peace.

"Nope." Charlotte popped the 'p".

"That bad that you can't figure out how to tell me?" Chance glanced down at Inessa, "Did we jinx ourselves?"

"I sure hope not." Inessa smiled up at him.

"Brace yourself." Charlotte paused a moment. "Joe died; thread died."

"Right…" Chance braced himself for monumentally bad news with how she stalled.

"Ariel says she feels Joe and I couldn't get much out of her before we sedated her, but she said she talked to someone. Their thread was always different due to their telepathic connection. Lucas and Kenzie's connection is similar. It's back. Not very strong and frayed all to hell, but it's there." Charlotte pulled her bottom lip between her teeth again.

Laughter filled the office. Chance bent over with his hands on his thighs. "We can't make this shit up."

"Chance?" "Dad?" The two women asked at the same time.

Chance wiped his eyes. "It's just been a lot today, Char. At least Nessa can help with this one." He pressed his lips to Inessa's for a quick kiss. "Keep me and your mom posted."

"Which one?" Charlotte's lips twisted into a smirk.

"The one that isn't going with you, smart ass."

Signal in progress…

Warren threw his head back against the wall a few more times. "What is happening to me?"

His arm jerked towards the screwdriver of its own volition.

We will protect you. Signal in progress…

"Gail. I need to find Gail." Code flew across the screen at a dizzying rate. Different camera angles popped up in boxes on the screen. "Where are you? I need you."

A small window popped up in the corner before it enlarged to fit the entire screen. Annie lying in a hospital bed nestled in James' arms. Abby sat on the bed next to their daughter's legs.

"Rest Annie. Everything will be okay." Abby squeezed Annie's leg.

"I don't know how, Mom. He tried to kill me. My own father tried to kill me. How is that okay?" Tears slipped down Annie's face.

"They are going to catch him, Anne. He's going to pay for what he tried to do to you." James kissed Annie's temple.

Abby cleared her throat. "I don't know what's going on with Warren right now, but something is clearly wrong. I wouldn't be able to function if Tal hadn't put the block up between us."

"I'm sorry, Mom. I know you love him." Annie's breath hitched with a sob.

"Easy Annie. You're right I do love him but I'm not going to let him hurt you or your brothers." Abby ran her hand along

Annie's leg. "Right now, you just need to get your strength back."

"Right. Rest. I just want out of this bed." Annie pouted.

"Soon, Anne." James tilted Annie's chin towards him and placed a soft kiss on her lips. "You are going to get out of this bed and do all of the things you always wanted to before you got sick."

"Sick. Disintegrating clone. Potato potahto."

James chuckled. "You know what I meant. You are going to live despite him trying to kill you."

The sound cut out on the video. Warren seethed from his spot in front of the computer. James was going to make him pay. He gripped his hair with his non-robotic arm. "Gail still loves me. I can fix this. I need to fix this. My baby girl. She's alive. My boys. I don't want to hurt them."

The robotic arm jerked towards the screwdriver again. It grabbed it and yanked it towards his chest.

"What the fuck?" He grabbed his robotic wrist and pushed against it. "What is happening to me?"

Signal in progress. Help on the way.

The sound returned on the video on the computer and zoomed in on James' face. *"He's going to pay for what he tried to do to you."*

"That's my daughter."

James' face contorted in anger and disgust. "He's going to pay."

"He's going to pay."

"He's going to pay."

Warren shoved the laptop away with his good arm. "Fuck you, James! That's my family."

"He's going to pay."

84

"Shut up!" Warren's scream echoed in the small unfinished room.

"I need help."

Signal in progress. Help on the way. All will be right.

"Nothing is right. God what is going on with me?"

Click. Whir.

The robotic arm jerked again towards him, hitting him in the face. His head bounced off the earthen wall behind him. Warren blinked a few times, dots danced in front of his eyes.

Click. The cybernetic appendage shot towards his throat and squeezed. Blackness crept into his vision. "No…" He choked out.

Warren wrestled with the arm that now had a mind of its' own. He felt around on the floor frantically with his regular arm to find anything that could help him. There was no way to reach Abby, but maybe hiding wasn't the best idea. Contact one of the telepaths. Yes. Lucas would help.

They are all the enemy. Signal almost complete. All will be right.

"Fuck." His fingertips slid over the handle. He gripped the handle to pull it towards him. Nothing felt right. He couldn't trust his own mind.

The hand around his throat squeezed tighter. A hoarse yell erupted from him as he swung his good arm towards the cybernetic one with the screwdriver in hand. The screwdriver embedded itself in the computerized arm just below the shoulder.

A pained cry escaped when the hand released his throat. Despite having turned off all the pain receptors in the arm they had somehow reactivated themselves. Waves of agony coursed through his body.

"What is happening to me? None of this makes sense."

Signal almost complete. All will be right. Infected to be eliminated.

"Wait! No!" Tears coursed down his face. With a better grip on the screwdriver, he stabbed the cybernetic arm repeatedly. Each swing brought on a new wave of pain that burned through his body.

"Lucas!" Warren screamed in his mind for the telepathic Exceptional.

"Warren?" Lucas asked cautiously.

"Help me. Please." Warren begged.

"We are..."

The telepathic connection severed. "No!" Something in the arm was able to control his ability to let telepaths into his mind. "This has to stop."

He slammed the shoulder of the cybernetic arm into the wall. All while repeatedly slicing into it with the screwdriver. Sparks flew out with each puncture. Warren gritted his teeth against the pain.

"You are not going to take my family from me." Warren continued to stab at the arm, not stopping when the piece below the elbow fell to the floor. A primal yell erupted from his chest. He slammed his shoulder into the wall a few more times and continued to pull at what remained of the arm with his good hand until it disengaged from his shoulder and fell to the floor.

Warren grabbed one of the pieces of his cybernetic arm and beat it against the wall. "Fuck you. You will *not* take my family from me. I will find you and kill you myself."

"Not anymore." He threw his back against the wall as he slid down to the floor.

Signal complete. Location of resistance base confirmed.

"Mom said he's got to be down here." Ilana moved down the earthen steps in front of Lucas. A small ball of fire danced in front of his sister to light their way.

"We've already checked the other two expansion areas, so this is the only one left. Charlotte and Inessa confirmed that he is not topside." Lucas pressed his lips together as they continued their descent.

"I know why you asked me to come with you, but I'm not sure if this was a good idea." Ilana reached the bottom of the stairs and stopped.

"Why would you say that? You are the best suited to assist." His brow furrowed.

"Um, yeah, maybe power wise but this *is* my father-in-law. He's already tried to kill his daughter and daughter-in-law. If this goes sideways, I'll have to tell my husband I kicked his father's ass."

Lucas chuckled at the smirk on Ilana's face. "We will have to hope it doesn't come to that."

"Let's hope so." Ilana looked each way down the earthen hallway. "Left, or right?"

"Let's try right first." The pair made their way down the hallway toward the area that was to become another section of housing units. Empty.

"Guess it's the other way then. What's down that way?"

"The new area for the hydroponics lab and a larger kitchen and cafeteria area." Lucas tried to reach out to Warren again mentally. Nothing but static came back.

"At least we are getting closer." Ilana started back down the way they had come from with her ball of fire.

"Lucas!" Warren's voice barreled into Lucas' brain.

"Warren?" Lucas asked cautiously, both out loud and mentally.

"Help me! Please!" Warren begged.

"We are coming to help." Lucas swore under his breath. A wall of static blocked their connection.

"What happened?" Ilana laid her hand on Lucas' shoulder.

"I had him for a moment and then the connection vanished. He was asking for help." A frown tugged down the corners of his mouth.

"That's good right? I mean if he's asking for help, he will go in quietly." Ilana looked as skeptical as Lucas felt.

"Unless it is some sort of trap." Lucas nodded his head towards the hallway. "We will not know until we get in there."

"Did you find him?" Talisa's voice entered both of their minds.

"I believe we are about to find him." Lucas replied but didn't hide the trepidation in his mental voice.

"Your father and I are on our way." Talisa came through insistent.

"Mama, I don't know about that. He's already going to be hostile with me. You and Dad might set him off more." Ilana didn't sound sure, but she was probably right.

"Ilana is right. Until we know what is going on with Warren, we don't want to incite his anger too much. He could cripple the network." Lucas glanced down the hallway they were about to go down. *"We'll keep you updated."*

"We'll send Chance down. Be careful." Talisa's frustration came through clearly.

"Ready?" Lucas squeezed Ilana's shoulder.

"I guess so." Ilana moved with him down the hallway to the open area that had been set aside for the cafeteria. The ball of fire moved behind them. It grew to illuminate their way through.

Warren was sliding down the wall missing an arm. Tears coursed down the man's face.

"Warren?" Lucas put his arm out to hold Ilana back. Ilana could handle herself better than most in the compound, but he still wanted to protect his sister.

"Lucas?" Sorrow and regret tinged the man's voice.

"It's me and Ilana. We're here to help." Lucas took a cautious step towards Warren. "What happened?"

"Holy shit! Warren what happened to your arm?" Ilana walked towards the man wide-eyed. She knelt next to him without a thought of her safety to begin assessing his injuries.

Warren jerked away from her. "Don't touch me! I don't know if I got all of it."

"Easy Warren. We're here to help." Ilana ran her fingers over the area where his arm that used to be attached. She jerked her hand back. "It's hot to the touch."

Lucas knelt on the other side of Warren. "We are not going to hurt you, Warren. What happened here? Did something attack you? If there is something loose in the compound, we need to find it."

"Me. I'm what happened" Warren whimpered with a wince as Ilana touched where his arm used to be.

"So, nothing attacked you?" Lucas furrowed his brow.

Ilana moved over to one of the pieces of the arm. She knelt to look at it.

"Ilana, don't!" Warren reached out towards her with his remaining arm.

"It looks like it's been used as a pincushion." Her fingers connected with the metal. A spark arked out from inside the remains of the arm with enough power for Ilana to yelp in pain. A burst of ice flew in the direction of Warren and Lucas.

Lucas threw up a shield of water just in time to block the assault. Layer by layer he built it up in order to protect them. "Ilana? Are you okay?"

"I can't stop it!" Ilana sounded panicked. Wind and sleet howled between them. Ice started to fill the room.

Ilana's distorted image flickered in and out of existence through the water shield that now started to freeze.

"I thought you were here to help?" Warren cowered against the wall.

"We are." Lucas responded dryly.

Ethan pushed his way into the room untouched by the cold weather swirling through the room.

"Ethan, I can't stop!" Ilana cried.

"Easy, Lana." Ethan made his way to his wife and set his hands on her shoulders. "Breathe."

"Why is she attacking us?" Warren's confused gaze fell on Lucas.

"I believe this is a malfunction with her powers." Lucas pursed his lips. Nothing was ever easy.

"And I thought mine was bad. I need to talk to Chance." Warren gripped Lucas' arm.

The wind and hail stopped as a brief burst of fire filled the room before it disappeared and left them all in the dark.

"Well, that was exciting." Charlotte walked into the room with her own ball of fire behind her.

"Ya think?" Warren looked up at Charlotte wide eyed.

Lucas lifted Warren on a cushion of water. He glanced over at Ethan holding Ilana, who had passed out. "Let's get everyone where they need to be. Warren is going to need medical attention once we get him to the holding cell."

"I need to see Gail. Please. And Chance." Warren gripped his hair with his remaining hand.

"You will, Uncle Warren." Charlotte inclined her head towards the hallway.

"Something tells me this is going to be worse than we thought." Charlotte's voice slipped into Lucas' mind.

"I believe you are right. He put up no fight. He's distraught." Lucas followed Charlotte out, pulling the water Warren rode on behind him.

"No joke, his aura is all over the place. We'll figure it all out though."

"Guys, I'm gonna take Ilana back to our unit." Ethan followed them up the stairs. "I'll check on my dad in a bit."

"Ethan. Son. I'm sorry. Tell your Mom I'm sorry, please?" Warren's grip on his hair didn't let up.

"Yeah. Sorry. I'll tell them." Ethan clenched his jaw.

"We've got this Ethan. Let us know if Illy needs us." Charlotte squeezed Ethan's arm and extinguished the fireball when they stepped out onto the main level.

Warren fell back onto the cushion of water curled up on a ball. "I'm sorry. God I'm sorry. I didn't know."

Lucas stayed silent as he maneuvered the water towards the containment area. He set Warren down on the bed in one of the units and pulled the water away from him. "Charlotte will be in soon to check your arm."

"I'm sorry, Lucas. God, I'm so sorry. I didn't know." Warren started to rock back and forth.

"We know Warren. We all are."

Abby stared at her reflection in the glass. Warren had yet to notice her. The tears had temporarily dried up. Not that one word wouldn't start them again at a moment's notice. The sight before her turned her stomach. Hunched over, disheveled, with the majority of one arm missing. Wires and a few charred circuits hung from his shoulder. Even though she knew it was his robotic arm, the urge to comfort him still lingered underneath the surface. She loved him. But to attempt to kill their daughter before they had a chance to know her trumped that.

"Why?" The near silent whisper deafened her. With no obvious response she pounded her fist against the impenetrable glass that separated them.

Anguish mirrored in Warren's eyes when he lifted his head. "Gail…"

"Just tell me why. Why would you try and murder our daughter just as we were about to get her back? What could possess you to do that?" Despite the urge to yell and scream at him, her voice stayed calm and even. Too calm.

"You've got this, Abby." Talisa's voice drifted into her mind. Of course, one if not both active telepaths monitored the situation.

92

"Do I? I want to hug him and strangle him at the same time."

"Which is why I am here if you need anything. We wouldn't let you do this alone or let you do anything you will regret later." The mental hug from her best friend helped her lock her spine in place for the emotional onslaught to come.

"Answer me, Warren. I need to know. Our daughter needs to know."

"My arm. There was something wrong with it. I would never hurt you or our children." Desperation tinged with regret echoed against the partition between them. It took considerable effort for him to sit up. Years of using his robotic arm as his primary had created a dependency on it. He stumbled twice before he made it to his feet. "You have to believe me Gail."

"What about Elan or James? Did you intentionally hurt them?" Abby folded her arms across her chest in lieu of meeting Warren's hand, now pressed against his side of the glass.

"They were trying to destroy our family! Those people…" He beat his fist against the partition. It immediately went to his head. His face scrunched up in pain. "No, that's not right. I don't…I can't…they hurt…I hurt…Gail, help me. Please."

A single tear cascaded down Abby's cheek. The agony and pain that contorted Warren's face tore at her heart. Was it possible something or some outside force influenced him? "I want to help you, but you need to help me understand what happened. You were so angry. So worried about James hurting Annie. Then you tried to stop them from bringing her back."

"Wait, you said tried to stop. Does that mean she's okay? Please tell me she's okay." Warren placed his palm against the glass. In any other situation she would have reciprocated from her side. This was but a minute taste of the hell that Talisa and Roark had been through.

Did she tell him? Should she withhold any information she had? He hadn't answered anything for her yet. If she dropped a nugget of information, would he reciprocate? Only one way to find out. "She's alive." She swiped away the tear that betrayed her and slipped past her control.

"Alive?" A sob shuddered through his body. "Please let me see her. I need to see her. I need to see the boys. I never wanted to hurt anyone. My arm…a virus in it…Steele…Gail, I love you and the kids…please…"

Her hand hovered of its own volition to meet his on her side of the glass. A virus? How long had it been there? Did she miss it when they created his arm? She had helped him create it. If she missed a virus, then she was at fault just as much for not catching it.

"Stop that, Abby. It's not your fault and if he's right it's not his either. We will figure it out." Talisa's voice cut off her own self-deprecating thoughts.

"Tal if he's right I should have checked for it before we attached it and installed his arm. That code has been a ticking time bomb for years."

"We won't figure that out right now. Lucas took the arm to a secure area. We'll see if Annie is up to looking at it once she's feeling better. Right now, just talk to your husband. Remember how guilty you felt when I put up the barrier between the two of you."

Abby mentally nodded, *"I was mortified by how I acted. Thanks, Tal."*

Warren's fingers flexed against the barrier.

"She can't right now. Annie came out of the pod too soon. There were complications." Her hand remained against the barrier.

94

"What kind of complications?" His voice shuddered, weak and raspy.

"The virus…it took your form and tried to kill Annie while she was moving back to her body from the laptop. We almost lost her again." Tears rippled through her voice.

Another sob wracked his body. "But she's going to recover, right?"

"We think so. She's resting with James."

"James…" The anguish quickly flipped to anger.

"Loves her. With every fiber of his being." Abby took a step closer to press her forehead against the barrier. "He will protect her with his life. The same as Elan and Ilana would with the boys."

"The boys can protect themselves."

"So can Annie."

"But he…he stole her from us when she died. He took her laptop."

"Warren, he's done everything in his power to help her." She shook her head, "I know part of this is still the virus and the other part is overprotective father instincts with his daughter. The only one that tried to kill her is you, on purpose or not."

"Jesus, Gail. I'm a monster."

"We are all what Steele created us to be in one way or another. We're all damaged and broken. But we are Exceptionals. We survive and we will get the opportunity to kill the bastard that did this to all of us."

"Abigail, what about us? I can't lose you too."

"Warren, I love you but…" But what? This was her husband, and he needed her help too.

"Please don't give up on us. I need you." Tears cascaded down his face.

Abby's heart constricted in her chest. "I'm not, Warren. We'll figure everything out." Even if figuring everything out meant things got worse.

"Annie needs you now too."

A few tears slipped past her control. "You both do. Chance is coming to talk to you soon. I need to check on Annie, but I'll be back."

"Thank you. I need to talk to him. Steele is coming."

Abby's eyes widened. "Fuck! Tal!" She yelled both out loud and mentally.

"We're on our way Abby."

Ethan cradled his wife too him as he entered their unit. He laid her down on the bed and retreated to the kitchen. Hopefully she would wake up soon. Whatever she had experienced was scary enough for everyone else, doubly so for her.

When he reentered the bedroom with a steaming mug of tea, he found her thrashing on the bed as if gripped in a nightmare.

"Lana!" Ethan set the mug down on the nightstand and sat next to her. He restrained her wrists gently. "Babe, wake up! Ilana!"

Ilana startled awake and immediately scampered back away from Ethan and stared at him wide-eyed. "Ethan? H-how…where…your dad…"

"Easy, Lana. Lucas and Charlotte have my dad. It's gonna be okay." He shifted towards her and tucked a lock of hair behind her ear. "Just breathe. Everything is okay."

"How? How is it okay? I could have killed your father and my brother." Tears streamed down her face. "Why are they doing this to me?"

"Shhh. It's okay." He hushed her in a gentle tone. Without making any sudden movements he scooted towards her on the bed. "We're gonna figure this out. Tell me what happened?"

"I...Lucas and I found your dad. Ethan, his arm. It was in pieces. It looked like it had been stabbed repeatedly." Ilana pulled her knees up to her chest.

"I saw the pieces when I came in the room. Your Mom said you might need me so I was focused on you. That was an impressive ice storm you threw at them." Ethan took her hand in his.

"I touched one of the pieces and a spark from it hit me. I didn't...Ethan, I didn't mean...I didn't want to hurt him or Lucas. Are they okay?" Her grip tightened on his hand.

"They are fine. They didn't get hurt from the ice. My father is fucked up, but that's another story." He leaned in and pressed a kiss to her forehead. "So, the spark hit you and then what?

"I don't know. The ice just started flying. I couldn't stop it. I couldn't feel it to pull it back." Ilana collapsed against his chest. "What's happening to me?"

"Honestly, I don't know but we will work through it together." He tucked her head under his chin. "You disappeared again." His arms tightened around her at the quake in her muscles.

"What?!" She pushed against his chest to see his face. "How...why..."

"Talisa told me. She was monitoring everything. It was like when you disappeared earlier, but this was more like flicking a switch on and off. You were here and then you weren't and a second later you were back." Ethan took her hands in his again. "What did you see?"

"Nothing changed. I don't remember disappearing. Just like before when you all said I was gone for an hour, I was there with Lucas and Warren and then you were suddenly standing in front of me. I didn't see you come in the room. Then everything went black." Ilana's head crashed into his chest, tears slipping down her face again.

"I've got you Lana." He dropped a kiss on the top of her head.

"How the hell are you supposed to help me? *I* don't even know what's going on!" A choked sob rolled through her body.

"However, I can. Whatever you need me to do." Ethan ran his hand along her back.

"*I* don't even know what I need. Are you magically going to know what to do suddenly?" Ilana snapped back.

A smile tugged at the corners of Ethan's lips. "There's my little spitfire." He kissed her temple. "One step at a time. Doesn't matter if that's one day, one hour, or one minute. I'm not goin' anywhere."

"I just want it to stop." Her body sagged against his.

"I know babe." He rubbed her back soothingly. "You said you think they are trying to kill you but what if it hurts because you're blocking what they are trying to teach you?"

Ilana yanked away from him, "You don't understand!"

Ethan shrugged with one shoulder. "You're right I don't. We've had this conversation, Lana. I have faith in you. Your parents have faith in you. Your brothers and sisters have faith in you. When are you gonna have it in yourself?"

"None of that matters." Ilana slipped off the bed to pace at the end of it.

It took a moment, but Ethan had to reign in the disappointment on his face. "It should. All you keep saying is you can't. Ya keep talkin' like that and you're right. None of it is going to matter. If you won't put the work in, then nothin' is gonna change and you're gonna stay miserable."

"How?" Her fists clenched at her sides. "How can I change any of it if I don't know what the fuck is going on?"

"Stop giving up, Lana." Ethan stuffed his hands in his pockets. One thing he knew 'bout his wife. If he continued to try and hug her, she would wind up punching him. "I need you. Your family needs you. I don't want to lose you."

"Oh yay! Everyone needs me, but no one can figure out how to fucking help me." Ilana yelled back at him.

"I love you. I know you can figure this out, but you are stubborn. What did Lucas tell you? Stop and take a minute to listen. You were gone for an hour and said you saw nothing. Because you don't want to see! If I could click my heels three times and make it all better, I would. All I can do is be here for you."

"Fat lot of good that is doing for me." She snapped back at him with venom.

Ethan closed his eyes and took a slow deep breath. He released it just as slowly and walked over to Ilana. His lips connected with her forehead, lingering for a moment. "I love you, Lana. I'll leave you be since I don't seem to be helping. Let me know if you need me."

"Ethan, wait! I didn't…"

"I know, babe. I'm gonna go check on my sister."

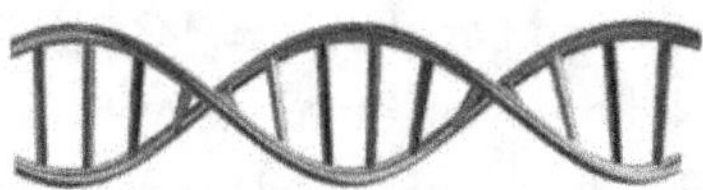

Talisa rushed down the hallway with Chance next to her. "How the fuck could Warren know if Steele is on his way."

"We won't have that answer until we talk to Warren. I have a feeling we aren't going to like the answer though." Chane crossed in front of her to open the door. "We'll get through it."

"You say that now. How the hell are we supposed to survive this? James is practically sewn to Annie while she recuperates, Ilana is having power malfunctions, and Lucas is trying to figure out if Ariel is losing her mind again." She threw both arms up in the air as she crossed the threshold. "This is a fucking disaster."

Chance chuckled, "Is there a partridge in a pear tree in there?"

"Now is not the time for jokes." She snapped back at him.

He gripped both her shoulders to stop her. "Kajah, we will get through this. We've made it this far. It won't be easy but, in the end, it will be worth it. Let's talk to Warren and then we will plan."

"We can't be certain." Talisa folded her arms across her chest.

"Nothing is ever certain. We both know that." Chance pressed his lips to her forehead.

"I don't know how you can always be so positive. That lunatic showing up here is our worst nightmare." She narrowed her eyes at him.

"I've been told it's part of my job description." Chance wrapped his arm around her shoulder. "Come on."

Talisa rolled her eyes at him. Abby stood outside of Warren's cell. Her arms wrapped around herself. She met Abby's eyes and wiped at her own chin to let Abby know she had chewed her bottom lip so hard that a drop of blood had slipped down her chin. "Abby, how are you holding up?"

Abby wiped her chin with her sleeve. "The boogie man is coming so it must be Tuesday."

"See? Even Abby is joking." Chance moved between the two women.

"If I don't, I'm going to cry." Abby ran her fingers through her hair. She inclined her head towards Warren. "He says Steele is on his way."

"And how do we know that?" Talisa knocked on the glass twice. Her stomach did a flip flop at the memories that surfaced just from looking at it.

A brief flash of anger flashed through Warren's eyes. His remaining fist gripped his hair. "Damn it, no!" He blinked a few times and grimaced. "He's on his way."

"How do you know that, Warren?" Chance had folded his arms across his chest. "We need to know."

"I sent the signal with the coordinates. He won't be long." Warren met Talisa's eyes, his own filled with sadness and remorse.

"Why the fuck would you do that Warren?" Talisa glared back at him.

"I didn't mean to." Warren hung his head.

"Didn't mean to? Please tell me something better than that. I didn't mean to eat the last piece of bread, sure. I didn't mean to tell the guy we've been hiding from exactly where we are so our whole family could be slaughtered? I'm not buying it." The growl that rumbled through Talisa's chest deepened when she felt Chance's hands on her shoulders. One glance at Abby softened the expression on her own face. "Sorry."

Warren's uninjured shoulder rose in a shrug. "I don't know how it got there but there was a virus in my arm. It must have been there since we built it. Dormant. A lot of it is fuzzy. It kept telling me that it would fix everything if I sent a signal. I had no clue what kind of signal. Just that it was supposed to help."

"You make it sound like your arm had a mind of its own." Talisa reached out and ran her hand along Abby's arm.

"It kinda did. Once I started the signal like it asked it tried to kill me with a screwdriver." Warren stumbled back to sit on the bed in the cell.

"Which is when you shish-ka-bobbed it?" Chance gave Talisa's shoulders a gentle squeeze.

"I guess, yeah. It wouldn't stop. The same message kept going repeatedly. Signal almost complete. All will be right. Infected eliminated. Until the signal completed and then it changed." Warren leaned back against the wall.

"What did it change to?" Abby laid her hand on her side of the glass.

"Signal complete. Location of resistance base confirmed. Lucas found me not long after that. I'd already removed my arm." Warren hung his head, "I can't apologize enough for everything. It was like a switch flipped when Annie got here. I was angry and I took it out on all of you."

"Trigger?" Chance looked down at Talisa.

"It wouldn't surprise me. Most of us had telepathic triggers when we first got away from Steele. We never thought to check for programmed triggers. Abby and Warren built that arm. Why would we think to check the programming?" She leaned back against Chance.

"It doesn't matter where it came from. I still did horrible things. I tried to kill my daughter. I attacked James and Elan. I made Abby physically ill to the point that it changed her personality until you intervened." Tears coursed down Warren's face.

Talisa pinched the bridge of her nose. "We've all done things we didn't really want to for Steele. It's what we do after the fact that matters." Her hand turned into a fist and pressed into her lips. Her stomach churned as the memories of her captivity rolled through her mind. She shook her head to clear it.

"Tal?" Chance cocked his head to the side.

She cleared her throat. "Warren, will you let me scan you?"

"Whatever you guys need." Warren scooted to lay flat on the bed.

"Tal?" Abby's turn to check on her apparently.

"Just covering all bases, Abby." Talisa waited until Warren closed his eyes and slipped into his brain. A lot easier when he wasn't actively blocking them out. She sped through as fast as she could without causing him discomfort. His memories of the recent events slipped into her mind. In all of them it felt like the logic and reason part of him had been locked away and the anger and resentment had been turned up tenfold.

"Warren?" Abby moved towards the glass at a grunt of pain from Warren.

"Open the door, Chance." Talisa blew out a shaky breath.

"Kajah?" Chance had moved in front of her.

"Not permanently, but let Abby see her husband. It should be left up to Annie but if he's up to it we're going to need Warren in the coming fight." A tear slipped past Talisa's control.

Chance opened the door to the cell and let Abby slip inside. He pulled Talisa close. His voice slipped into her mind. *"Too familiar?"*

"You could say that. The arm took over his mind. His anger was turned up way past even what they wanted for James. He's going to need time to heal, but we're going to need him." Talisa wrapped her arms around him and leaned her head on his chest. *"Tell me we're going to beat this son of a bitch Sani."*

"That's the plan, Kajah. That's the plan."

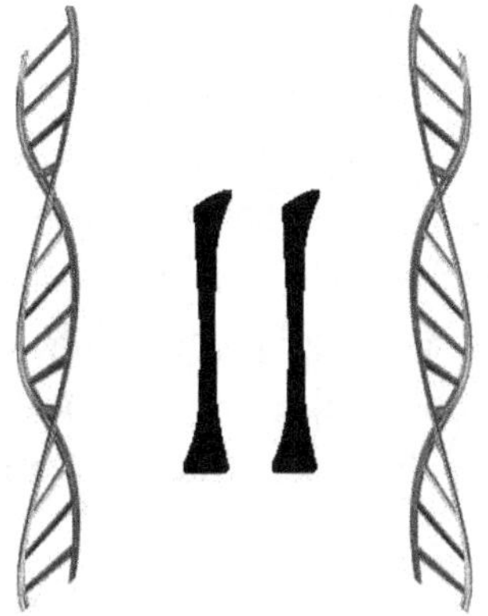

Lucas walked from the kitchen to the small sitting area in Ariel's apartment. "Here, drink this."

Ariel took the steaming mug of tea from him. "Thank you, Lucas."

"Mom, what happened? You looked terrified and then you passed out." Mackenzie met Lucas' eyes, worry in her own.

"Joe…" Ariel screwed her eyes shut and shook her head. "Kaliya."

"Easy, Ariel. We know this is hard. Take your time. Drink your tea." Lucas felt for his mother-in-law. To go from thinking her husband was dead with their connection severed to feeling it again with someone else on the other end had to be disconcerting.

"You two have got to be so tired of having to constantly take care of the crazy one." Ariel sipped the tea and let out a shaky breath.

"No, Mom. Don't ever think that. We don't mind at all." Mackenzie ran her hand along her mother's back. "We don't think you're crazy."

"Not at all." Lucas knelt in front of the two women seated on the couch. "Just take it slow. Who is Kaliya?" She stared into her mug for what felt like an eternity. No need to rush her through it. Lucas knew how difficult the situation was for her. For the last year she had been under the impression that Joe had died and now, somehow a small piece of him remained. He knew how he would feel if it had been Mackenzie.

"She's…with Steele." Ariel glanced back and forth between him and her daughter. "Said he had done experiments on her."

"Are we sure it's not a trick, Mom?" Mackenzie reached out and squeezed Lucas' hand.

"Positive. The kind of connection your father and I had is like the one that you two have. It happens with telepaths. It's different than the mate connection." Ariel lifted the mug to her lips, her hands shaking.

"That connection broke when Joe died and suddenly it's back?" Lucas squeezed his wife's hand back. "From what you've shown me, I do not believe that it is a trick. Steele may be able to manipulate DNA, albeit poorly, but he would not be able to reproduce the connection."

"Well, he did something." Mackenzie's brown furrowed.

"The experiments. He…he…" A choked sob escaped from Ariel, "grafted Joe's DNA onto Kaliya." She set the mug on the end table and moved around Lucas to pace the room. "He stole your father from us and took what was left of him and…and…"

Lucas shot back to his feet when her fists clenched at her sides. The last time she had been this angry things were thrown around the room and then she had been out cold for two days. It had been a year since that occurred. "Breathe Ariel. We will figure this out."

"Breathe? Breathing isn't going to fix this. Breathing isn't going to change the fact that they took bits and pieces of my husband and grafted what was left of him onto someone else. She said many successful experiments. Who the fuck knows how many other poor souls he stole from and gave to her. So, I can "feel"," Her fingers came up in air quotes, "my husband but it's not him. Doesn't remember me, Kenzie or Tori. Please tell me how we are going to figure this out."

"Welcome back, Mom." A small smile tugged at the corners of his wife's lips.

"I don't know, Ariel." Lucas leaned in and kissed Mackenzie's temple. "But we will do everything we can to figure it out."

Ariel rubbed her temples. "Little girl, if you think this is back, we may need to have you checked out."

A full smile spread on Mackenzie's face. "You haven't felt much besides depression and despair since Daddy died. I'll take a little anger especially if it gets you back in the fight."

"Okay, we've established that what I'm dealing with is beyond fucked up." Ariel moved back to the couch to drink more of her tea. "What is going on in the compound? I'm not listening to thoughts, but I can tell the whole damn place is in turmoil."

Lucas chuckled with a smile of his own. He knew his mother-in-law well enough to know that when she wanted to change the subject that was it. "There have been a myriad of issues going on. As you know my parents are back. They returned just as Annie died."

"Annie?" Ariel glanced at him quizzically.

"Abby and Warren's daughter." Mackenzie answered.

"When did they have a baby? I haven't been out of it that long." Ariel's eyes widened in shock.

"Steele. He made a disintegrating clone. She jumped into a laptop and my parents created a new body for her." Lucas sat on the coffee table in front of them.

"I'm sorry I asked." Ariel set the mug down and scrubbed her hand over her face.

"There has been a lot going on." Lucas shrugged, "Always is though." He paused for a beat. "We just arrested Warren and put him in a containment cell."

"Who the hell is running security and making sure the perimeter is secure?" Ariel leaned forwards towards Lucas. "Wait what happened with Warren?"

"Steele." Lucas and Mackenzie answered in unison.

"Can we kill that man more than once? I swear to God, if I ever get my hands on him, it will be slow." She glanced at her daughter. "And don't tell me I'm back just because I'm plotting to kill Steele."

Lucas shook her head, "We wouldn't dream of it."

"Chance is dating someone." Mackenzie cringed.

"About time." Ariel squeezed the young woman's arm. "Is she nice? Do you like her?"

"Inessa and the Chief are good together. They seem happy together. They only had a brief stumbling block when Charlotte realized that Inessa was her other mother." Lucas took the now empty mug and set it on the kitchen counter.

"Nope. That's it. I'm done." Ariel pushed on her knees as she stood up. With no other indication of her intended destination, she walked towards the bedroom.

"Mom?" Mackenzie shot to her feet.

"Ariel? Can we help with something?" Lucas wrapped his arm around his wife's shoulders.

Ariel shooed them away with her hand. "I'm sorry I asked for an update. You guys go do what you need to."

"Mom are you sure?" Kenzie moved towards her mother.

"Positive. I'm going to take a shower. I'll be fine. Love you both."

"Love you too, Mom." Mackenzie worried her bottom lip. *"Lucas is she really, okay?"*

"For now, I believe she is. She's not wallowing or crying. Rightfully so, she's angry." He pressed a kiss to her temple. *"I think she's on her way back to us."*

"You look more comfortable now that you're dressed." Abby shifted the table that held the finished tray of food away from the bed.

"Definitely more comfortable than having my rear end exposed." Annie smiled and snuggled into James.

James gently kissed Annie's temple. "Shouldn't be too much longer and you'll be able to get out of here."

"I hope so." Annie picked at the hem of the blanket that covered her. "How did it go with Warren?"

Abby cleared her throat, "Fine. The situation is contained."

"Mom? Did he hurt you?"

"Not the way you're thinking. The whole situation hurts, but your father didn't do anything to hurt me." Abby concentrated on Annie's fingers picking at the hem. What could she tell her daughter that wouldn't upset her? Being manipulated by Steele, she would understand. Hell, the virus causing everything she would even get. But they weren't announcing that Steele knew where they were yet.

110

"And yet you still look like you want to vomit." Annie smirked at her.

"She's not wrong, Abby. You don't look so hot." James laid his hand on top of Annie's to stop the nervous picking.

"Just tired. Emotionally and physically. It's been a long few weeks." She squeezed Annie's leg. "We think we know what caused it all. Just need to make sure it is all contained."

"What do you mean contained? I thought Warren was in a cell." The familiar scowl returned to James' face.

"He is."

"Mom, what happened? Come on. You know we're going to find out anyway. I'd rather hear it from you." Annie laced her fingers with James'.

Of course, they weren't going to let it slide. In for a penny, in for a pound. Abby took a deep breath and let it out slowly. "You already know that Warren's one arm is robotic. There was an accident years ago and he lost his arm. Your father and I built the prosthetic together. Did all the programming and created the technology to attach it seamlessly. We did it when we were working for Steele."

Annie blew out a breath in frustration. "So, you're about to tell me that Steele did something to it and it wasn't really him?"

Abby nudged her daughter's leg, "Too smart for your own good, young lady. Yes. Steele implanted a virus in the coding. We think it triggered when you first got here. We won't know until we get a look at the code and Warren is in no shape to look at it right now. Talisa has cleared him on the mental side."

"Son of a bitch." Annie swore and clenched her hand into a fist.

"Anne?" James pulled Annie closer to him.

"How can I be mad at him, James?" A tear slipped down Annie's face.

"You have every right to be mad at him Annie. I am. I still love him but I'm

furious about what happened." Abby's heart constricted at the sight in front of her. The mixture of anguish, fear, and blinding anger that came off the pair in waives made sense. Hell, everyone that knew so far felt betrayed. She pushed a hint of calm into the room.

James' gaze snapped toward her. A low growl rumbled through his chest. Annie pulled his gaze towards her. "Are we just going to believe it was a virus that was dormant all this time?"

Abby surveyed the other side of the room instead of watching her daughter distract James with a kiss. "We won't have all the answers until what's left of the arm is inspected."

"Hey sis! How ya feeling?" Ethan chuckled. "Pretty good I guess if you're kissing him in front of Mom."

Annie buried her head in James' chest. "Hi, Ethan." came her muffled response.

"Don't embarrass your sister, son." Abby chuckled. If Danny walked through the door, she would have all her children in one place for the first time.

"Hey, I've got to catch up on picking on my baby sis. She's as red as a dang tomato." Ethan grinned.

"He's fine, Mom." Annie cleared her throat. "I'm sure I'll find a way to get him back."

"After watching Annie's memory videos, I see they were pretty accurate." A genuine smile peeked through. Even with all the chaos around them seeing her children like this brought her joy.

A sad smile marred her daughter's face. "Yeah, they were."

Without notice, alarms started to go off across the room. Abby slipped off the side of the bed, the previous joy dissipating into concern. "Let me see what's going on."

"Abby?" James sat up straighter.

"Not sure. This happened earlier. We never did find out what caused it. She's still in a medically induced coma." Abby grabbed the pad next to the bed. Each reading more puzzling than the one before it. She grabbed a pen light and shone it in each of the girl's eyes. Did the little girl just wince?

"Tal, not like we need something else right now, but something is happening with the little girl. Alarms started going off." Abby focused on Talisa.

"I'll be there as soon as we can. I'm with Chance trying to come up with a plan. What are the readings saying?"

"Blood pressure spiked dangerously high and then went dangerously. Her heart rate hasn't changed, oxygen levels have increased, and I swear to God, she winced when I checked her eyes with the pen light. Both are equal and reactive. Her saline bag is low. I'm going to change that."

"Thank you. I'll be down soon."

The alarms quieted as the girl's levels came back to normal. Abby blew out a breath and changed the saline bag. She adjusted the medication keeping her in the induced coma.

"Mom?" Annie's voice startled her.

"Sorry guys. I'm not sure what's going on." Abby hit a few buttons on the pad to record what she had done.

"That was weird." Ethan folded his arms across his chest.

"It's like she was trying to push through the medicine. Almost like she was trying to wake up." Abby pursed her lips.

"Could this day get any weirder?" Annie asked.

"I think you just jinxed us, Anne." James smirked at Annie.

"Stranger things have happened." Abby sighed and set the tablet back down.

"Stranger things have happened." Abby sighed and set the tablet back down.

Danny wandered the halls of the compound for an hour. Part of him wanted to go see Annie or talk with his mom, but he really wanted to talk to his wife. Both his mother and sister had been through enough in the last few days. He stood outside the door to the training room now bracing himself for what he would walk in to.

Elan and Chaz's training sessions tended to be brutal. He pushed the door open and stood off to the side to watch. Despite how aggressive it got watching the way Elan moved was beautiful. Danny knew his wife was a trained killer but seeing her in action reminded him of how lethal she could be. Not just with the poison that came out of her claws, but with the grace of her movements. Even with as fast as Chaz moved, he couldn't escape her attacks. Elan knew how to improvise. Chaz's movements were more deliberate as if they had been choreographed for him. The pair stopped sparring and looked at him. Chaz sped over and stood in front of him.

"How is training going?" Pride welled up as he looked at the man in front of him. Not too long ago, he would only sit like an animal. Seeing Chaz standing on two feet was a definite sign of progress.

"Not too bad." Elan walked up and gave him a quick kiss.

"I'm glad to hear it." Danny kept the smile plastered on his face. His wife looked so relaxed that he didn't want to ruin the moment.

"What's wrong?" Elan folded her arms across her chest.

"Nothing. Why?"

"You think your wife can't tell when something is going on with you?" She smirked at him. Chaz stood there and nodded back at him.

Danny blew out a frustrated breath. His wife knowing something was wrong was one thing, but Chaz knowing left him a little unsettled. "They caught my dad. He's in containment."

Elan's expression softened. "Danny…are you okay?"

"I guess. I mean I think so. It needed to happen. Probably should have happened after he attacked you and James. Something's not right with him though." Danny leaned back against the wall behind him.

"Crazy." Chaz interjected.

A chuckle escaped from Danny. Chaz had a unique grasp way of seeing the world. Most things were black and white to him. After seeing the attack on Elan, it made sense that Chaz would think Warren was crazy. Especially since he had defended them by turning his father into a giant pinata. "Yeah, that's part of it."

"What do you mean, something is not right? We know he was going bat-shit with everything going on with your sister." Elan laid a hand on his shoulder.

A frown sucked away the brief respite from the reality of everything happening. "He ripped his own arm off. Stabbed it off. Got more holes than Swiss cheese."

Confusion danced across Chaz's expression. The man tugged on his own arm. His expression changed from confusion to horror. "Why?"

"One of my father's arms was robotic. He didn't rip off his flesh and blood arm." Danny scrubbed his hand over his face. Explaining it didn't make him feel any better.

"But he's contained now?" Elan squeezed his shoulder.

"He's contained. In a cell. My father is in a cell." Danny clenched his jaw. "Everything is so messed up. I don't understand it. He was fine before Annie got here."

"Trigger, maybe?" Elan's frown matched his own.

"No clue. Probably. Who knows. I should probably check on my mom and my sister, but Mom has been so messed up and Annie's recovering." Danny wrapped his arm around Elan's shoulder. He needed contact with his wife. Chaz still looked confused. He had no idea if the man comprehended what they were talking about.

"Steele." Chaz said matter of fact. Perhaps he had a better grasp than he thought.

"Everything seems to tie back to that lunatic. It's as good a guess as anything." Danny nodded.

"If Annie is recovering then our parents should be able to work on it." Elan managed a small smile for her husband.

"I guess. Just waitin' for another shoe to drop. It's never one thing at a time around here." Danny leaned in to kiss his wife's temple. "I'm sorry if I interrupted with this."

"We were finishing up." Elan shook her head. "There's always going to be something else Danny. It's the world we live in. Until Steele is gone, we are always going to be looking over our shoulder."

Danny chuckled when Chaz looked over his shoulder. "I guess you're right. Guess I just wonder what it would be like to not live like that? As long as I can remember, it's been like that. Would be nice to get to some semblance of normal."

"This *is* our normal babe. We haven't gone out for another retrieval for supplies or located another Exceptional since Annie got here, but I'm sure we'll get back to that soon." Elan shrugged. "You going to go see him?"

"Who? My dad? I don't know. I thought about it. Maybe after Annie does. Maybe Ethan will want to go with me." Danny stared at the ground. "Not even sure what I'd say to him. He's done some pretty messed up stuff."

Elan pursed her lips, "I'll go with you, if you want me too."

"Appreciate it, babe. I'd understand if ya didn't want to be around him at all after he attacked you. I'll see what happens after Annie sees him. She's got more baggage with him than I do. He attacked my wife and brother-in-law. He tried to erase her from existence. Literally."

"Whatever you want to do." Elan ran her hand along his back.

"Okay. Enough of that depressing crap. Time for you two to hit the showers and eat something." Danny hugged Elan to him.

"Tori." Chaz stated plainly.

Danny grinned at Chaz, "I'm sure Tori will be by to see you. Might be a better visit if ya shower first though."

"Danny, that's not a good idea. Tori doesn't understand." A deep V etched between Elan's eyes.

"Tori understands enough. Chaz isn't going to hurt her." Danny turned them towards the door. "Just trust me on that."

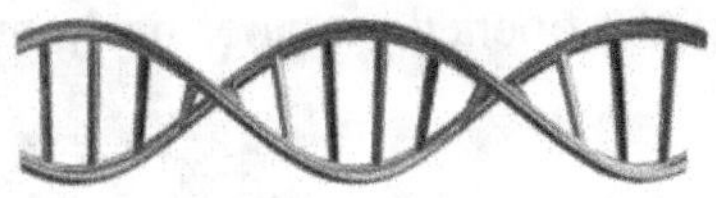

118

Ilana rolled her shoulders in the hope that it would help with the headache that had taken root at the base of her skull. Fresh air. Maybe that would help. She really wanted to talk with Ethan. Would he even want to talk to her after she had pushed him away? "Wonderful Guardian I am."

The woosh of their door closing behind her pushed her forward. Topside. That's what she needed. Space between her and everyone else. The corridors were eerily quiet. A flash of light caught her attention out of the corner of her eye. She turned her head towards it. It flickered and disappeared. Ilana blew out a frustrated breath and continued towards the tunnels that lead to the surface.

The door that would lead to a few brief moments of freedom stood in front of her, some unseen force stopped her from going through it. Perhaps it was the pounding in the back of her head. She looked over her shoulder and down the stairs that led back into the compound. Perhaps it was something else. Ethan said she should trust her instincts.

"I mean why not? Of course, it feels like something needs my attention back down there when I want to go outside for fresh air." Ilana pressed her lips together in a thin line.

Another light caught her attention, but this on appeared as a ball of light that hovered in front of her. "What is that?" She reached out and ran her fingers through the light. It bounced in front of her for a second, flickered out of sight and reappeared a few steps down. It blinked out of sight and came back again, this time another few steps down.

"Follow the bouncing ball of light. What could go wrong?" Ilana sighed and started down the stairs with the glowing orb. It grew larger when she opened the door back into the main area of the compound.

"Maybe I feel asleep and I'm dreaming?" She pinched her own arm as hard as she could and winced. "Nope, I'm awake."

The globe of light bounced and flickered in and out of sight as it made its way through the hallways of the compound. It paused at one of the cross sections and stopped. It bounced and flickered again as if it was looking both ways before it started towards the new area that had been put together for bringing Annie back and housing the other pods that had been brought back from the compound Steele held her parents' prisoner.

Ethan should be down here. He went to see his sister. Maybe it was directing her towards him to work things out. Was it trying to show her something? Why didn't the Spirits just talk to her and tell her what they wanted from her?

The globe stopped outside the door to the lab. It bounced a few times, then disappeared. "What the hell?" Ilana paced outside the door wringing her hands. "Am I losing my mind?" She stopped in front of the door again, took a deep breath and pushed the door open.

Annie laid on the bed curled up next to James. Ethan stood next to Annie's bed, staring in the direction of his mother. Abby stood over the little girl they had taken out of the pod to create Annie's body.

"Lana?" Ethan took a step towards her, "Babe, you okay? You look like you've seen a ghost."

"Ethan...I..." She chewed on her bottom lip, "I'm not sure." Her gaze shifted to the little girl again. The globe reappeared and hovered over her. "You guys see that, right?"

"See what, Ilana?" Confusion was evident on Abby's face.

Annie and James looked equally confused but didn't say anything. "The light above the girl. It's hovering above her. I followed it here." Ilana crossed the room to the young girl.

"I don't see any light above her." The confusion on Abby's face shifted to concern.

"It's right there." Ilana stuck her hand into the light.

"Lana, we don't see any light." Ethan moved towards her cautiously. "Some alarms went off before, but no lights."

"Alarms?" Ilana shook her head, "No. There's a ball of light right over her. I followed it through the compound, and it led me here."

"The Spirits, maybe?" James piped up from his spot next to Annie.

"Why am I the only one that can see it?" Ilana looked up at Ethan, fear in her eyes.

"Easy, babe. We'll figure it out. James is right. Maybe they are trying to tell you something." Ethan glanced over at his mother and then back to Ilana.

"You don't believe me." Tears burned at the back of her throat.

"That's not it at all." Abby jumped in. "We're concerned. If that's what you are seeing, then there must be a reason for it. Ethan is right. We'll figure it out."

Ilana's eyes went wide as the globe lowered itself into the chest of the little girl. Alarms rang throughout the room. "What is happening?"

Abby grabbed the pad again, her eyes going wide. "Ilana, what do you see? Her vitals are all over the place."

"The orb. It went into her chest and then the alarms went off." Ilana clung to Ethan's side.

"Mom?" Ethan pulled her close and kissed the top of her head reassuringly.

"I don't know, son. Talisa should be here any minute." Abby checked over the girl.

"She's glowing." Ilana stared at the little girl. "Her whole body is glowing." She pulled out of Ethan's arms and laid her hand on top of the girl's. The sound of the doors opening behind her startled her, but she didn't turn around to see who it was.

"Glowing?" Talisa walked up to the table taking one of the other tablets. "I'm not sure there's a medical cause or treatment. This sounds spiritual to me. But I think you're right Abby. She's waking up."

"Mama…" Ilana's blinked a few times. Everyone in the room flickered from sight and were replaced by their own orbs of light. Then everything went dark.

Talisa heard Ilana call for her, but her concentration remained on the pad in front of her. "One second Ilana." Every read out was more confusing than the last. None of it made sense.

"Lana!" Ethan's yell filled the room over the alarms.

"Where did she go?" Abby's concern caught Talisa's attention.

"What the fuck?" Talisa looked around the room. Ilana had disappeared again. They needed to get to the bottom of this. Once was a fluke, but two times was cause for concern.

"Ma? Where the hell did she go?" James slipped off the bed next to Annie and had moved towards them looking around cautiously.

Talisa pinched the bridge of her nose. "James, take your girlfriend for a walk."

"But Ma." James protested.

"No buts. Go. Scoot. Too many cooks in the kitchen. Abby, Ethan, and I can handle this. Annie must be going stir crazy. We'll want to look her over later to ensure everything is as it should be but right now get out." Talisa waved her hand towards her son.

"James don't argue. I can leave this room. We will check in and see if they need anything later. We can't do anything for Illy right now." Annie slipped off the bed carefully. She wobbled and grabbed the railing to steady herself.

"Be careful Annie." Abby's level gaze stayed on her daughter.

"I will Mom. Don't worry I promise not to blow him up if I go to see him." Annie managed to smile. She grabbed James' arm to keep her balance as soon as he was close enough.

"We appreciate that, Annie. We might need his help. Supposedly Steele is on his way." Talisa met James' eyes. *"Do not go off half-cocked son. We will need his help when Steele gets here."*

"Easy, Anne. Don't rush it." James wrapped his arm around Annie's waist. *"I won't. Call us if you need help finding Illy."*

Talisa nodded her head. "Let's see if we can get those blasted alarms to stop going off? Ethan you okay over there?"

"I tried to turn them off earlier but none of the options on the pad helped." Abby went back to check the little girl's vitals.

"Is this like earlier? She's just gone." Ethan gripped the handle on one of the nearby rolling carts.

"No idea. Chance and Lucas were with her last time. She was there and when they turned away, she vanished. Last time she was gone for an hour." Talisa closed her eyes and took a deep breath. She reached out to Chance. *"Sani got a minute?"*

"What's wrong Kajah?" The concern carried easily through Chance's mental voice.

"Ilana disappeared again, the alarms are going off with the little girl we put in an induced coma, and we're waiting for

a madman to show up. Chaos as usual." Talisa continued checking over the little girl.

"The last time the alarms went off like this was when Ilana disappeared before. At least I think the timeframe matches up." Abby grabbed a syringe and dispensed the medicine into the IV.

"Lana wasn't down here then so we don't know if the glowing globe of light thing happened then too. She's the only one that could see it." Ethan folded his arms across his chest.

"Wait. Around the same time?" Talisa pursed her lips at her best friend's nod. *"Make that the alarms going off again. Apparently, it happened the last time Ilana disappeared. And Ethan mentioned something about a glowing globe of light."*

"It's got to be connected somehow but I don't know how. Glowing globe? Let me meditate and see if I get anything."

"Illy was the only one that could see it. Not sure if that means anything." Talisa scanned the room and focused on the spot Ilana had been standing in. "I can't feel her anymore. Just like the last time."

"I know she needs to learn something, but can they teach it to her without taking her away like this? She's not in the best mindset." Ethan's frown matched her own.

"I don't have answers for that, Ethan. It's like she's disappeared from existence." Talisa swept her hair back into a ponytail.

"No time went by for her last time. She was gone, what an hour? All of this is scaring her." Ethan rubbed his hands over his face. "Come on, Lana. Come back to me."

"I'm sure she's trying Ethan." Despite Talisa's calm façade, internally she was scared.

"Easy, Tal." Abby's mind filtered into her mind. *"There has to be a reason for this. Isn't that what you've always told me about the Spirits?"*

Talisa blew out a breath. *"Easier said than done. This hasn't ever happened before."*

"She'll be back. We must believe that. Didn't she come back exactly where she disappeared from last time?" Even though Abby spoke to her mentally she continued to work on the little girl.

The alarms stopped just as abruptly as they started. "Well, that's one thing." Talisa looked over the readouts on the pad. All had fallen back within normal range. "You're right Abby. She's pushing to wake up."

"Great…what does that mean? How does a little girl, who is all of what five or six years old, wake herself up from an induced coma?" Abby checked the girl's pupil response again.

"How does my wife disappear from existence and reappear like nothing happened?" Ethan asked wryly.

"Touché, son." Abby chuckled. "You would think we would stop being surprised at some of these things."

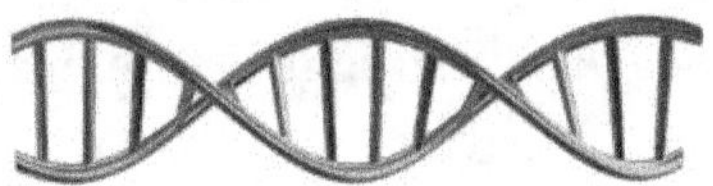

Tori lifted her hand to press the button on the door. It opened before she had a chance to touch it. "Hi Danny! I came by to see Chaz. You're definitely looking better than the other night."

"Hey Tori. You sure this is a good idea. Chaz isn't like other guys."

"Hmm, I hadn't noticed." Tori said with a quick roll of her eyes. "I know he's not going to hurt me." She laid her hand reassuringly on Danny's arm. "I'll be fine."

126

A breeze flew between them followed by a snarl. "Caiman's."

Tori giggled and reached up and touched Chaz's cheek. "I know Danny is Caiman's. I came to see you."

Chaz leaned in and sniffed along her wrist. He moved up along her arm to her neck, eliciting another giggle from Tori.

"Chaz." Danny sighed and shook his head. "You can't just go around sniffing people like that."

Chaz pulled back and looked at Danny quizzically. "Why?"

An amused smile twitched on Tori's lips. Her hand came up to cover her giggle. Danny was correct. Chaz was different, but for some reason she felt safe with him despite all she had heard about him.

"Ya just can't. Most people won't understand it." Danny raked his hand through his hair.

"Why?" Chaz asked again.

Tori stepped up and placed her hand on Chaz's arm. If she let this keep going the two men would just go back and forth and she could tell Danny struggled to explain. "It's usually reserved for couples in private."

"Couples?"

Tori chewed on her bottom lip as she tried to come up with an answer that would end the questioning that obviously made Danny uncomfortable. "Mates, like Danny and Caiman."

Chaz gave a nod to indicate he understood.

"Why don't we go in your room? We can relax there." Tori took a step towards the door to Chaz's room.

Without a word Chaz blurred away towards his room.

"Tori…be careful." Concern was etched on Danny's face.

Tori lingered a moment to reassure him. "Don't worry I will. We're just going to talk. We'll be fine. I'm going to see if I can get him to nap. He doesn't sleep enough."

"Yell if ya need anything." Danny walked into the kitchen.

Tori entered Chaz's room and heard the shower running. She picked up the pillows on the floor and placed them on one end of the couch. A few stray pieces of stuffing were strewn in one corner. She grabbed them and the offending pillow and stuffed the pieces of cotton back in.

After rummaging through a few drawers, she found a sewing kit and sat down on the couch to repair it. Chaz came out and watched her but didn't say anything. He sat next to the couch on the floor. She knew she wouldn't break him of that behavior overnight.

"Fix?" Chaz tilted his head to the side.

"Yes, I'm fixing it." Tori finished the last few stitches and tied off the end. She clipped it with the small scissors and set the kit on the end table. "See, all better."

"Better?" Chaz's nose wrinkled in disgust. "Why?"

"Why what? What's wrong?" Her eyebrows drew together in concern.

"Alarms."

Tori looked towards the door and shook her head. "I don't hear anything. It must be in a different part of the compound. If the main alarms aren't going off, then we should be okay." She tilted her head to the side and studied him, "You can hear it though. Your hearing is excellent."

"Yes." As per usual his answers were short and to the point.

"Why don't you sit up here with me?" Tori patted the cushion next to her. Chaz stared at her but didn't move. "Remember before? You feel asleep up here with me."

Chaz climbed up on the couch next to her and sat back on his legs. "Here."

This would take a lot more work than she had anticipated. She reached up and trailed her fingertips along the spots that graced his temple. "You don't have to if you don't want to. I just thought you would be more comfortable."

A low purr rumbled through Chaz's chest eliciting a smile from Tori. "You help?"

Tori nodded, "I'm here to help."

"Help." Chaz sniffed up along her arm and nuzzled her neck.

"Right. Help. We're friends." Tori stayed still while he continued his. Her fingers danced along the fur-like hair along the nape of his neck.

"Tori friend." Chaz pulled back and studied her with a serious expression on his face.

She continued to run her fingers along the back of his neck and shoulder. The continuous purr rumbling through his chest felt like a good sign. "How was training?"

"Intense. Caiman good fighter."

"Caiman is a really good fighter. So are you though." Tori pulled her hand back to tuck a lock of hair behind her ear. The purr shifted to a low growl. "Did you not want me to stop?"

Chaz gave a curt shake of his head.

"Did you get any sleep last night?" Instead of answering he looked down at his hands. Tori cupped his cheek, "Hey, it's okay if you didn't. I won't go anywhere if you want to nap." The creases in his brow told her exactly how concerned he was about her leaving.

"You stay?" The concern on his face shifted to concentration.

Tori worried her bottom lip debating her next move. Danny wasn't wrong. Chaz was different. He scrambled off the couch when she stood up. "I'm not going anywhere. Just grabbing some of these pillows." With a few in her hand she laid them on one end of the couch. She stretched out on the couch and beckoned him over.

Chaz crept over to her, each step cautious. "Stay here?"

"I'll stay here with you. I can see how tired you are after training." When he reached the couch, she reached out and cascaded her fingers along the spots at his temple. "We'll nap together."

One eyebrow quirked up. He was obviously skeptical. "Tori help?"

"Yes, I'll help you nap." A smile spread across her face as he crept up onto the couch next to her. He stretched out and the purr resumed as his head nestled against her chest.

Annie leaned against James for support. Her strength hadn't returned as quick as she had hoped. Apparently the first thing on her agenda with her newfound freedom happened to be facing off with the man that tried to kill her. Her father. What do you say to that? Even if it wasn't his fault, it still hurt.

"Anne?" James kissed her temple.

"Hmm?" Annie tilted her head up to kiss his lips. "Sorry. Guess I got lost in my own thoughts."

"What's going on in that beautiful mind of yours?" He smiled down at her.

"Wondering if this is a good idea. I know I'm going to have to deal with him, especially if Steele is on his way." She leaned her head on his shoulder.

"Do you not want to do this right now? We don't have to." James waggled his eyebrows at her, "We could always find something else to do."

Heat rushed up from her chest to her cheeks. A shy smile tugged at the corners of her lips. "What did you have in mind?"

James stopped them in the middle of the hallway. He tilted her chin up and met her eyes, "Whatever you are comfortable with. Anne, I'm not pushing you to do anything you're not ready for. If you want to see your father, then we'll do that. If you want to go back to our unit and curl up on the couch and just enjoy the fact that we can touch each other, we'll do that."

"I love you, James." Annie lifted her hand to caress the side of his face. She guided his mouth to hers for a deep searching kiss. A sigh escaped into the kiss at the feel of his arms around her, holding her close.

James pulled back just enough to touch his forehead to hers. "I love you too, Anne." A genuine smile graced his features.

"Let's get this over with. Then we can worry about other things. Like getting you into the training room to blow off some steam before you explode." She brushed her lips across his.

"Anne, I'm fine."

One side of her mouth tilted up in a smirk. "Now that I'm back in my body, I can completely feel how much you need it."

James' smirk matched her own. "Okay, smart ass. But only so you don't worry."

Annie laced her fingers through his and started towards the containment cells. "I will worry regardless."

"You ready?"

"As I'll ever be." Annie stepped into the room. A brief flash of the memory from when she first got here, and James showed her the containment area popped into her mind. It never occurred to her that she would be coming back here to visit her father.

"The second you want to leave we will."

"Thank you." She let out a sigh as she stared at the cell that held Warren. A few of the fabricated memories that Steele had implanted played through her mind. All good ones with Warren. A tear slipped down her face. James tenderly wiped it away before she could.

He leaned in close to her ear, "I've got you."

Annie stood in front of the glass staring at her father. Pitiful didn't cover it. Disheveled, destroyed, and total despair came to mind when she looked at him. A lump rose in her throat at the sight. Most of the anger dissipated. She knew exactly what it was like to be manipulated by Steele. How could she dismiss the fact that her father had been manipulated too? "Daddy," came out in a hoarse whisper.

"Deep breath." James squeezed her shoulders from behind.

She cleared her throat, "Daddy." It came out stronger this time. Warren didn't move from his spot huddled in the corner.

James reached over her shoulder and banged on the glass, "Warren. Your daughter is here to see you."

Warren jumped at the sudden noise. He glared at James; anger marred his features. His whole face contorted in pain, and he shook his head roughly. "Annie? Baby?" Tears streamed down his face. He shambled over to the glass and pressed his hand to it.

Annie reciprocated. Tears welled up in her own eyes. "Daddy."

"Baby. I never wanted to hurt you. I am so sorry. God I am so sorry. I don't blame you if you hate me. A virus. It was a virus."

All Annie could manage was a nod. She leaned back against James for strength.

"Please you have to believe me. I hate myself for not catching it." Warren leaned his head against the barrier.

"M-mom told me. It doesn't surprise me that Steele would drop a trojan horse like that. Do you need anything?" Annie's heart ached watching this broken version of her father.

"I'm so happy you're alive. That it didn't work." Tears continued to course down the man's face.

"We are too." She glanced up at James with a small smile. Annie took a deep breath and focused back on her father. Time for the harder questions. "Daddy, how much time do we have?"

"You can stay as long as you want, baby." Warren leaned against the glass to help keep him upright.

"I know. I mean for Steele. How long until he gets here? We need to prepare." She pulled James' arm around her waist and leaned back against him.

"I…I don't know for sure. I think I managed to encrypt it but I'm not entirely sure. My arm was trying to kill me at the time." Sadness, remorse, and disgust flickered through Warren's eyes.

"I'll take a look and see if I can get anything from it that will help." Annie laid her hand on top of James' "Open the door please."

James' jaw clenched at her request. "Are you sure?"

"Positive. He's not going to hurt me." She pressed her lips to his, lingering for a moment. "I promise."

The click of the door opening startled Warren. Annie walked as fast as she could into the cell. She touched his shoulder and winced at the sight of the charred circuits and wires hanging where his arm used to be.

Warren spun around and threw his remaining arm around her. "Annie…my baby…I'm so sorry. God, please forgive me."

Tears coursed down her face as she hugged him back. Despite the fact that she couldn't see James, she could feel how tense he was. "It's not your fault, Daddy. It was Steele…it was me."

"What?" Warren and James yelled in unison.

Annie didn't let go, only hugged her father tighter. "It was me. I was the trigger. I was the one that set this all off."

"Anne…" James placed his hand on her shoulder from behind.

Warren pulled back enough to wipe away the tears on Annie's face. "Annie, this isn't your fault."

"We're all what Steele created us to be. He created me to destroy you and I did that. Maybe not how he intended." She took Warren's and James' hands in each of hers, "I did cause a lot of problems."

James shook his head with a sigh. "She's not wrong. We've all been manipulated by Steele in one way or another."

Annie leaned up and kissed her father on the cheek. "Try and get some rest. I'm going to go look at your arm and check the encryption that went out. We'll see you soon."

"Be careful, Annie." Warren frowned as he looked between her and James.

"I'll protect her with my life." James pulled Annie close.
"Thank you." Warren nodded in James' direction.

Inessa hummed to herself as she navigated the hallways. Chance had been occupied with the impending attack from Steele. A cursory glance at the threads she could see told her that everyone in the compound was healthy at least. Even

Warren's thread that had been easy to find before due to how frayed it had become had been repaired.

Her brow furrowed at one thread though. Although normal for a thread to occasionally pulse brighter it typically only did it once or twice and then returned to its normal state. This particular thread continued to pulse brighter and brighter.

She stopped in the middle of the hallway and focused. One by one the other threads faded into the background. The one left veered off behind her into several different directions. "Must be one of the Nashuk family."

Inessa let the other threads come back into focus, so she didn't make herself dizzy. Step-by-step she followed the pulsing thread through the compound. She tilted her head to the side when she realized it went into the makeshift lab that had been set up.

"None of this makes sense." Talisa's voice drifted into the hall when Inessa pushed the door open.

"I'd say that's unusual, but it's really not." Abby drew blood from the little girl on the table.

"So, another day with weird occurrences in the compound?" Inessa smiled brightly as she entered the room. She continued to follow the thread to the spot where it ended. "Huh…"

"Inessa?" Talisa raised an eyebrow in question "Not that we're not glad to see you but what's up?"

"That is the weirdest thing." Inessa circled the spot the pulsing thread stopped at.

"We're chock full of weird shit right now." Ethan scrubbed his hand over his face.

Inessa waived her hand back and forth across the spot where she would expect a person to be standing. "So weird."

Abby chuckled, "Care to elaborate there?"

"Well, I was just walking down the hallway and took a quick peek at the threads in the compound," Inessa paused and glanced at Abby, "Warren's are repairing themselves. They aren't frayed anymore." She grinned and lifted up on the balls of her feet as she shifted her attention back to Talisa. "I saw one that was pulsing brightly. Totally not normal. I mean once or twice sure when new bonds are formed or a current one is strengthened…"

"Inessa, the point?" An exasperated Talisa snapped.

Murky greys and reds pulsed out through Talisa's aura. The woman before her was tense with fear and skeptical as hell. Inessa giggled nervously, "Sorry it's something new and weird. I'm going to have to talk to Charlotte about this one. Anyway. I followed the pulsing thread down here and it ends there. A person should be standing right there."

"My wife was until she vanished." Ethan's muted blue told her just how moody the young man was.

"Wait Ilana vanished again?" Inessa's eyebrows knit together. She tilted her head to the side and let all the other threads drop out of sight, focusing solely on Ilana's. It continued to pulse until it flashed so bright that it almost blinded her. When the brightness died down it went from its normal luminescent white to gold. "That's odd."

"Odd? What about my wife's thread is odd? I mean other than her thread being in the room when she ain't." Ethan's aura shifted through a myriad of colors at once.

"The thread changed colors. I've never seen that happen before. A strong bond is usually white. Her's just turned gold." Inessa pursed her lips while running all the possibilities through her head, but no explanation came to mind. Something else she should compare notes with Charlotte about.

"And that means?" Talisa waved her hand at Inessa indicating she should continue.

"Honestly…no clue, but as far as I can tell she's right there. Other than the color it was like that when she disappeared when she was with Chance. Another plane maybe?"

Talisa's aura pulsed with streaks of grey, pink, yellow, red, and violet. Her fists clenched at her sides. With her head tilted back and looking at the ceiling she let out a primal scream. "Bring her back right now!"

"I would say I've seen weirder things, but I think they are all on par with each other lately." Abby flashed the pen light in the little girl's eyes again and sighed.

"Something wrong Ma?" Ethan stepped forward. He immediately hopped from the spot Ilana had disappeared from.

"In the middle of everything else we're trying to figure out how this little girl is breaking through a medically induced coma and forcing herself to wake up." Abby swiped her finger across the screen of the tablet she held in her hand.

Inessa focused on the little girl. She followed a thread from the girl to Talisa. Several more went from the girl to somewhere else in the compound. One thread in particular that came back towards the girl held specks of black throughout a frayed grey. Her aura pulsed white, then spirals of beautiful greens and violets spun through it. "Uh Tal…you brought her back with you right? She's already very connected to several people in the compound including you."

Talisa smoothed her hair back, "I know."

"One thread is fading. She's never been awake here though." Inessa let her normal psychedelic vision come back into focus.

"I'm not surprised by that." Talisa bit the inside of her cheek.

"O-okay…" Inessa's eyebrows knit together in a frown.

"Do you see anything else Inessa?" Abby looked up from the pad.

"She's definitely working towards waking up. From the green I can tell she's healing and very peaceful. The violets tell me she is very spiritual and wise. Most of her aura is white. I rarely see that much balance in a person."

"And all that means…" A hit of fear slipped into Talisa's aura.

"I can't tell you more until she's awake."

"So, we're back to square one." Abby sighed.

"Feels more like a damn hamster wheel Ma." Deep grey that signaled skepticism spiked through Ethan's aura.

"Well, can whoever is running on the damn wheel stop and give me my daughter back!"

Talisa took a deep breath and let it out slowly. She unfurled her clenched fists and set the pad down.

"Tal?" Abby sent a wave of calm through the room with her inquiry.

"I just need a minute." Talisa waved off any concern as she walked into the small office area that had been set up. With the door shut she moved in front of the window that had been installed so they could see into the lab area. She pressed her hands to the glass and closed her eyes. Each breath in and out calmed her more.

A clear picture of Ilana remained her focus. If she was actually in that spot but in another plane, then theoretically she should be able to see her if she concentrated hard enough. She winced as an image of Roark on the other side of the partition flashed in her mind. It flickered away but came back just as quick as it had gone.

"Tal?" Roark stepped up to the glass. As they did often to approximate closeness, his hand pressed to the glass. "You all right in there?"

140

"Just missing you." She set her hand against the glass opposite his. "Call it wallowing, if you want."

"I wouldn't, because that would mean I wallow, and men don't wallow." He winked and leaned closer.

A shudder ran through her at the memory. She focused again on Ilana pushing to find her with her telepathy. Something. Anything that would let her know her daughter was okay. Talisa filtered through all the brains in the compound. Not one of them had been Ilana. Another flash of light brought more of the memory with Roark back to the front of her mind.

"Li, baby. Wake up." Roark pressed his hand to the glass in their usual morning greeting. "You know you don't want them to wake you."

Talisa sighed and pressed her hand against his where it lay on the other side of the glass. Tears filled her eyes, but she blinked them away fast so their captors couldn't see them. She forced a smile. "Morning, hot stuff."

"Ready for a brand-new day?"

Talisa chuckled to herself. She really was an odd one but after a year of being held captive by a lunatic. Seeing Roark every day but never being able to touch him? Anyone else would have gone batty. For some reason it calmed her. Gave her better focus. She didn't know if it had to do with how they survived in there or some variation of Stockholm Syndrome, but it helped. Maybe it had to do with her desire to gut the asshole that had done this to them all.

Each memory that flashed in her mind focused her more. Flashes of Ilana moved through her mind to replace the memories of captivity. Little by little everything around her faded away.

Ilana stood just as she had been when she disappeared. White orbs danced around her. Each one stopped in what felt like a designated spot forming a circle around her. The first orb transformed into her father. The next her mother. Chance's parents followed. Her grandparents. Every orb fluttered and took on the shape of one of their ancestors or one of the fallen Exceptionals. As if they were taking turns to speak with her daughter. To impart some wisdom, some knowledge.

Ilana stood there stock still. Not one hint of acknowledgement from her. She wasn't hearing them. Safe but not listening.

No wonder Ilana had power malfunctions. Only two of her powers came from being an Exceptional. The rest came from the Spirits and being a Guardian. They were withholding her power until she listened to them.

Now that she knew that Ilana was with the Spirits, only one option remained. Time to get back to work. With a hard tug she yanked the band holding her ponytail in place. With the ponytail holder between her teeth, she ran her fingers through her hair. Once she had gathered it at the back of her head again, she secured it and pulled the door open.

"Tal?" The wave of calm from Abby worked its way through the room again.

"I'm fine Abby. Careful with that calm you keep putting in the air. You're going to put me to sleep." Talisa grinned at her friend. Did Inessa run off?"

"Inessa went to go help Chance…or find Charlotte. I'm not entirely sure what she was talking about both when she left." Abby chuckled, "Sorry, the calm cloud was more for Ethan. He's about to rattle apart with worry for Ilana."

"Can ya blame me Ma? My wife keeps disappearing." Ethan paced at one end of the room.

"Well, this tidbit should help. Ilana is with the Spirits. Let's hope she listens and comes back to us." Talisa scooped up the pad and scrolled through the readings. The sigh of relief that came from Ethan diffused the tension in the room. "I'd say about an hour before she's awake. What do you think Abby?"

"That's what I'm thinking too." Abby nodded, "Neil is on his way down to help out. I'll go check on Warren when he gets there if that's okay."

"Of course. Lots of moving parts going on right now." Talisa smiled at her friend.

"It's no wonder we're all so good at juggling them."

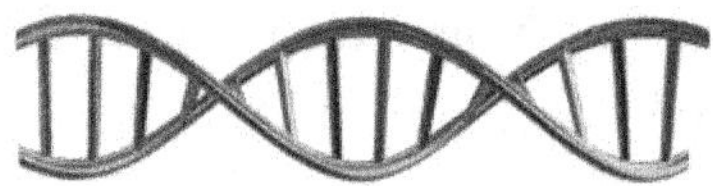

Once Lucas and Mackenzie left her room Ariel had taken a long hot shower. She'd cried, yelled, screamed, and collapsed to the floor of the shower sobbing. The water had long since turned cold when she managed to pull herself up. The wallowing had to stop. Hell, she'd been doing it for a year. She knew no one begrudged her for it, but it needed to end.

Ariel ran her fingers along the back of her neck. Right over the spot she felt the connection. The low tingle that in the past had always let her feel Joe. *"Kaliya..."*

Nothing. Not even the bounce back of the connection she had felt earlier. Despite the appeal of having even a small piece of Joe around it wouldn't surprise her if she scared the poor soul off.

Instead of wallowing she started to clean up her unit. The kids had done some surface cleaning, but she couldn't remember the last time her unit had been deep cleaned. After about an hour she stopped when she stumbled upon one of the photo albums they had managed to save. She curled up on one end of the couch with Joe's favorite blanket and flipped through the pictures.

"Ariel. It pleases me that you are okay. You disappeared quickly the last time we spoke." Kaliya's voice filtered into her mind.

Tears welled up in Ariel's eyes. The connection felt bittersweet now. *"I'm so sorry about that Kaliya. I'm embarrassed to say I fainted."*

"Please do not apologize. I can understand it would be a shock. You are well now, though?"

Ariel couldn't help the smile that formed. She knew it wasn't Joe but just feeling a little bit of him was comforting. *"I am, thank you. I've been looking through an album of Joe with the girls and me."*

"You are all very beautiful. I remember from the images you showed me last time we spoke. May I ask you something?" Kaliya sounded nervous.

"Of course, you can. Please don't feel nervous. We're both adjusting to this." Even if Steele had done this to Kaliya. It wasn't her fault.

"I had a dream after we spoke. I was diffusing a bomb. You were telling everyone to get back. You called me Tiger. I said I love you and the bomb went off."

Ariel didn't have enough presence of mind to block her shock from the connection. Tears welled up in her eyes again. *"I am so sorry Kaliya. I had that nightmare again before we spoke for the first time. It's how Joe died."*

"But it was not from your point of view. It was from Joe's. I felt his panic. His regret. His love. My question, is what were Joe's gifts? If you don't mind me asking." Kaliya's genuine concern for Ariel came through.

144

"He had amphibian like gifts. He could breathe underwater and could regenerate. He also had extremely sensitive derma." Ariel wiped at the tears that had escaped.

"I see. Those are some of the gifts I was given. Ariel, I know this will sound odd, but I feel connected to you. Not just because of this mental connection. More than that. I must sound crazy."

A sniffly laugh escaped, *"Not at all. I feel the same way. I'm glad you don't think I'm crazy."* She flipped back a few pages in the photo album in her hand. *Would you like to see what we were like? I was looking through some pictures."*

"I would like that."

The images started to play through their connection like a slideshow. Pictures of Joe with the girls as they grew up lingered longer than others. It stopped on an image of Joe and Ariel kissing on their wedding day. Ariel cleared her throat. *"I'm sorry, Kaliya. I haven't looked at these in so long."*

"Please do not apologize. That was your wedding day. You threatened him if he got the cake all over your face." Kaliya made the statement as if she had been there.

Ariel inhaled a sharp breath, *"H-how? How do you know that? I didn't say what it was from."*

"I do not know. I could just see it in my mind. You were beautiful that day. He called you Ari." Kaliya confusion came through the connection as well as her sincerity.

"A-are you getting Joe's memories Kaliya? I mean I guess that could happen if you got his regeneration. It would depend on what they used to graft his gifts on to you." Ariel flipped to another picture of them together. *"Do you get anything off of this one?"*

"I'm sorry Ariel, I don't. I apologize if this hurts you."

Ariel shook her head both physically and mentally. *"Liya don't apologize. It's okay. We'll figure it out."*

Tension reverberated through the link. *"Kaliya? I'm sorry if I overstepped. It just sounded right. I didn't mean to offend you."*

Silence echoed back. Disappointment gnawed at her. Ariel knew it wasn't Joe but talking with Kaliya had been comforting and now she had offended her. She flipped the book closed and tossed it on the coffee table.

"Ari, I'm sorry. I couldn't let them figure out I was talking to you. Orders have come down. A signal has come in."

"Orders? I don't understand. What kind of signal?" Ariel wrung her hands together. She couldn't lose Kaliya too.

Another pause in their conversation. Ariel started to pace in front of the couch. "Come on. Come on. Please be okay."

"It makes me happy that you worry for me. They are decrypting the signal, but it is supposedly the location of the resistance headquarters. We will be attacking." Worry carried through Kaliya's voice.

"Fuck. Um…that's where the girls and I are. My whole extended family. I didn't exactly want to meet you on the battlefield." Ariel continued to pace. She needed to talk to Chance.

"I apologize Ari. I have to go now. You and the girls please be safe. I will contact you as soon as I can."

"Be careful, Kaliya. Please."

"One more thing…I don't mind being called Liya."

The connection fizzled to the tingle at the base of her skull. Ariel needed to go find everyone and let them know.

Charlotte poked her head in Warren's office with a smirk on her face. It shouldn't surprise her that Annie would jump right into things the moment she had been released from the lab. "Shouldn't you be resting?"

Annie hit a few keys on the laptop in front of her, "Didn't I rest enough before I died? When you think about it, that's all I did when I was trapped in the laptop too."

"Okay, smartass. You know what I mean. No one would begrudge you for taking your time before you jumped in on something. You literally just came back from the dead." Charlotte pulled a chair closer to the desk.

"Do we have any other computer experts lying around?" Annie tilted her head in Charlotte's direction. "Besides, I can't sit still right now. Not with Steele on his way."

"Where's James? I'm surprised he let you out of his sight." Charlotte leaned back in the chair. James leaving Annie's side definitely surprised her. He'd barely left her side since he accepted their connection.

A genuine laugh escaped from her friend. Annie sat back in her chair. Code continued to run across the laptop screen at a dizzying rate. "I'm kind of surprised he did too. Apparently, my reasoning made sense to him. I set him to the training room with your father."

Definitely Warren's daughter. Computer work never stopped. "He probably needed to beat something up even if it is Dad."

"At least your father heals. James has been practically sewn to me since the whole mate thing came up. Don't get me wrong I'm not complaining but he needs to get the pent-up energy out or he's going to explode."

"True." The code on the laptop appeared to stop scrolling and as far as Charlotte could tell it ran backwards before stopping again and going forward again. "What are you working on in here anyway?"

"My Dad's arm. Well, the coding in it. He did encrypt the message but not at his usual level. It only took me five minutes to get through it, so I expect it won't take Steele's idiots much longer." Annie focused on the screen again. The little bit of humor deflated from her.

"So, sooner rather than later. How are you holding up really? Dying and coming back to life aside you've had a lot to deal with since you woke up again." Charlotte leaned forward and laid her hand on top of Annie's.

"Ya think?" A hollow laugh escaped from her friend. "When I woke up, I was determined to hate Warren. Seemed pretty cut and dry since he tried to kill me. Logical right?"

"Of course, it is. We all wondered what the hell happened to him. It was the weirdest damn thing." Charlotte knew the whole situation hurt Annie deeply. She showed up here and found not only her family, but a mate, and then she dies, and her father tries to stop her from coming back to life.

"All logical until you find out that you're the reason for the whole Jekyll and Hyde routine. It was a trigger in the code. Buried so deep I can see why he never found it. Buried in, I lost count on how many subroutines down that I lost count." Tears welled up in Annie's eyes.

Charlotte grabbed a tissue from the box on the desk and handed it to her. "Wait Aunt Abby and Uncle Warren built that arm while they were still working for Steele. That was way before my mom became patient zero."

Annie wiped at her eyes. "Talk about the extra-long game. Almost fifteen years. There were two separate triggers in there. One for a male child and one for a female child…me. They were specific."

"How specific?"

"The one for the male child was programmed for Hunter Warren Johnson. And the female one for me. I did this." Annie leaned elbows on her legs with her head in her hands.

"Wait. Back up. What do you mean *you* did this?" Charlotte placed her hands on Annie's arms.

"I was the trigger. Me showing up here triggered the personality changes in my dad. The skepticism of me and the aggression as soon as the mate thing came up. It turned him into the asshole he was acting like." Annie raised her head and slipped her hands into Charlotte's.

"Holy shit! Annie, that's a heavy burden to put on yourself." She wanted to comfort Annie. What did you say to any of this though? So, what if you turned your father into a raging bastard? Not exactly a Hallmark moment.

"It's all there in ones and zeros Char. Yes, he did try to kill me but how can I be mad at him when I'm the reason he flipped his shit? And he didn't just hurt *me*. His rage made my mom physically ill. He attacked Elan and James. He wouldn't have done any of that if it wasn't for me. How do I tell any of them that this is all my fault?" Tears slipped down Annie's face.

"Uh you don't because it's not." Charlotte smirked at her friend. Why were all the smart people in the compound so dense sometimes?

"Char, it's there in black and white."

"Uh huh. You told me it's in the code that *Steele* placed a virus with a trigger in Warren's robotic arm almost fifteen years ago. Did you write the virus?"

"Um…no."

"Did you pick the names?"

"Well, no. Of Course, now I just feel weird about my name."

"Okay. Then how is any of is this your fault?"

"Not directly but I'm the one that set everything off."

"Yup ya did." Charlotte sat back and looked smugly at Annie.

"Charlotte! What the hell?" Annie slammed upright into the chair.

"Annie, you may have set it all off, but you are the one that's solving the mystery. When everyone hears that you confirmed the trigger was planted by Steele fifteen years ago, they will understand, and they won't be mad at you or Warren." She bit her bottom lip, "Elan might take a little longer but that's just Elan."

"I'm not sure how you made any of that sound logical, but you did." Annie laughed.

"It's a gift. Besides if I didn't talk you out of your downward spiral, James would have found you here all weepy and snotty. The second he saw you, he would have wanted to beat the crap out of something again."

Annie stood up and hugged Charlotte. "Thanks Char. Even I'm starting to feel a little jittery."

"We've got a brief respite. Go topside and look at the full moon." Charlotte hugged Annie back. Now that Annie had settled, she needed to go back to looking for Ilana.

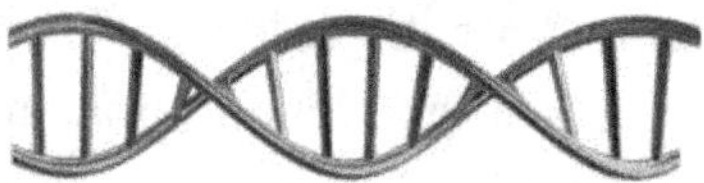

"We've got it." Steele stormed into Taylor's research area. It had taken years, but he finally had the information he needed to locate the Infected. He could be rid of that bitch Talisa, and her whole Infected family.

Taylor examined Kaliya on one side of the room. When he entered the room, she paused what she was doing. Every time she looked at him with poorly masked distain, he wanted to be rid of her. Her mind wasn't even half as good as Talisa's, but he would have to make do with what he had. "Got what sir?"

"The location. Well, we will once it is decrypted. Where are the damned computer guys. They aren't in their office." Steele scowled as his gaze traveled up and down along Kaliya. He shuddered internally. It didn't matter how effective it had become; the extra infection had given her less than human characteristics. Scales formed around her temple and ran down around her ear to her neck where small gills had formed.

"Hello, General." Kaliya bowed respectfully. It didn't even hide the stub of a finger in its hand. They had cut it off to test its regeneration. It looked grotesque.

Steele waved his hand dismissively. "Whatever. How is *it* doing? Everything progressing as you expected?"

Taylor nodded but never made eye contact with him. "As well as can be expected. The regeneration is not as fast as I would like but we are getting better results from grafting brain matter instead of hair or skin tissue. Unfortunately, I don't have the donor's medical records to compare regeneration rates to."

The monster they created sat perfectly still on the lab table. It stared off into space paying both him and Taylor no mind. It was almost like the moment he waved his hand it turned off or something. He gestured towards it again. "What's wrong with it? Does it have an off button?"

Taylor rolled her eyes at him, "No sir. You've been very adamant that Kaliya refrain from speaking to you unless asked a direct question. She is following your orders."

Steele rolled his eyes right back at her. He would never understand why she insisted on giving that thing a name and treating it like a person. "More importantly, back to my original question. Where are the desk jockeys? We need to prepare to attack."

"General I run the research department. I am not privy to the whereabouts of staff members from other departments. If I were to hazard a guess, I would say in the mess hall, the bathroom, or changing shifts." Taylor's tone was patronizing.

Without any warning Steele charged Taylor and shoved her into the nearby filing cabinets. He wrapped his hands around her throat and squeezed. "Remember your place, girl. You are nothing without me. You do *as* I say *when* I say it."

Taylor clawed at his hands around her throat. Watching this woman struggle as the light in her eyes dimmed exhilarated him. She didn't know her place. Didn't understand the order of things. She would though. He would make sure of it.

He remembered they weren't alone. A glance at the lab table told him that *it* was about to intervene. The moment was ruined.

Just as quickly as he had grabbed her, he released her and smoothed out his jacket. A lingering ruddiness in his cheeks were the only indication of what had transpired. He inclined his head towards Kaliya. "Make sure it's ready to fight."

Taylor's rasping coughs receded behind him as he strode out of the room. He threw the door open to the computer lab and found one man in there. "Decided to come back to work, did you?" No one in the complex had the dedication of his original team. A shame really that they all became infected.

"I just came on shift, sir. What can I help you with?" The man scrambled from his seat and stood at attention.

"What's your name?" Steele waved his hand dismissively as soon as he asked. "Never mind. I don't actually care. We received a signal from the Infected base. You need to decrypt it now so we can eliminate them."

"Y-yes sir. Right away sir." The man bowed respectfully in Steele's direction. Then he just stood there. Why on Earth would he just stand there? Shouldn't he go straight to work on it?

"What the hell are you waiting for?" Steele blustered. "This is priority number one. Why are you still standing there?"

The man's eyebrows disappeared into his hairline. "Sir, I would be happy to work on it. There's one slight problem though."

"I don't want to hear your damn excuses. What is it with your generation? Do you even know what the meaning of hard work is? My original research team, they understood what it meant to be dedicated to a cause." A scowl crept across his face.

"What happened to them sir?"

"They were infected. Best minds in the world and they became those damn Infected. Now I need to find them and kill them. You son are going to help me do that. Do you think you can focus and decrypt the message so we can go and eliminate them? Not too much to ask hmm?" Steele glared at the young man who appeared to be shaking. Why did half the ones he recruited after Roark have such a weak constitution? The one in front of him looked like he either wanted to vomit or pass out.

"N-no sir." The man stuttered.

"Then get to work damn it." He shook his head in disgust. Good help had been so hard to find.

"S-sir…"

"What?!" Steele snapped back at him. "Why are you still standing there?"

"I…uh…need the message to decrypt sir."

Steele grimaced. Yes, he would need the actual message to work on. He patted the pockets of his jacket. "Ah, yes." Once he felt the lump of the flash drive, he pulled it out of the inside breast pocket. "Here you go."

"Thank you, sir. I'll work on this right away."

"Yes. Yes. Good work. Bring it to me as soon as you have the location."

Ilana blinked a few times and took in her surroundings. What the fuck? This was not the lab. Where the hell was she? Wait a minute. The old ramshackle barn that held their plane gave the first clue. How did she end up topside? The last thing she remembered was following a glowing orb down to the lab where Annie and the little girl were. Talisa walked in and that was it. What the fuck was happening to her? And why was she so tired?

"Ilana!" Talisa's voice slammed into her mind.

"Mama, what happened?" Ilana winced and wrapped her arms around herself. She trudged towards the houses so she could get below ground again.

"We don't know baby. You vanished again. This time, Inessa even followed your thread down here like you were still in the room.

"Still in the room, but I'm not still in the room." None of this made any sense.

"Where are you now?" The concern was evident in Talisa's voice, but she didn't sound panicked.

"I'm topside. I don't know how I got here." Ilana stopped at the low stone wall and looked up at the sky. *"There's a full moon."*

"I'm not entirely sure what happened, but I'm sure the Spirits had something to do with it." Talisa paused for a moment. *"A full moon is a good omen."*

"How long was I gone this time? Why would they take me and still not speak to me? I don't understand." Ilana continued her trek through the house and down to the tunnels. If she acknowledged her mother's mentions of omens the conversation would go on longer.

"You were gone a few hours. You sound tired baby."

"I'm exhausted and I don't know why." Ilana snapped unintentionally at her mother.

"I'm here if you need me." Talisa's voice faded into the back of her mind.

Ilana allowed a brief glance over at Warren in the containment area as she passed through. The sight of her father-in-law bubbled up a pang of guilt. She had disappeared again, and Ethan might have needed her. The door whooshed open to grant her access to the common area. Maybe she was hungry, but she really didn't know. Sleep. She felt like she could sleep for a week.

"Thank the Spirits you're okay." Charlotte ran up to her and pulled her into a hug.

"I'm fine, Char." Ilana immediately stiffened up in her sister's embrace. Everyone else being worried about her made her feel weird. They shouldn't need to worry about her. She was supposed to be the all-powerful Guardian. What a joke.

Charlotte took a step back, looking her over. Probably with her doctor brain. "I'm just glad you're back. Can I do anything? Do you want anything? I could go get you something to eat or drink. Maybe Pops or Lucas have a tea that will help you decompress."

"I just said I was fine, didn't I? So, I'm fine. I don't need anything. No food. Nothing to drink. No tea. The last thing I need at the moment is visions on top of disappearing." Ilana snapped at her sister.

"I'm sorry Illy. We were all just really worried about you. I mean this was the second time this happened."

Her sister looked at her with concern and pity. It made Ilana want to vomit. Why did none of them see the issue here? The Spirits were trying to take her power away from her. Not them. Her. They were trying to kill her. Not everyone else. Just her. "Look, I'm sorry I worried everyone. I don't know what or why this is happening. When I figure it out, I'll let everyone know. Until then, there isn't much anyone can do. Anyway, I guess Inessa followed my thread down to the lab and it looked like I was still here."

Charlotte tilted her head the way she did when she was studying someone's threads and auras. Her eyes went out of focus for a brief second, then she chewed on her bottom lip. A telltale sign she was mulling something over before she said it. "Well, that's new."

Ilana's eyes rolled towards the ceiling. "Oh my god, just tell me. It can't be any worse than the random disappearing acts." Did she really want to hear whatever this was? Not really. But she knew Charlotte. She wouldn't leave it alone.

"For starters, your aura is a damn rainbow. Little bit of everything in there. Not entirely unusual. It happens sometimes, but yours looks like it's fighting itself. Kind of like James' aura after Annie's body died and she jumped into the laptop. The mate connection was seriously confused."

"Is that it? I'm a rainbow?" Sleep. That's all Ilana wanted right now, and her sister stood in her way.

"Yeah…yeah…I can see your exhausted. No, it's your thread. It's gold." Charlotte's expression remained serious.

"And that means what exactly?" Great another thing to figure out if she survived this.

"That's the thing. Not a clue. I have no idea. I'll ask Inessa if she's seen it before, but this is new territory for me." Charlotte did the only thing she could do. She shrugged.

"I can't process this right now Char. I'm sorry I can't. If you find something out, great, tell me. If not I'm not sure I can handle anything else. I'm going back to my room to lie down." Another pang of guilt crept in. Ilana knew her sister only wanted to help. Like her parents wanted to help, and her husband, and her siblings…and…and…and. Nothing but answers would help now.

"I get it, Illy." Charlotte pulled Ilana towards her in a fierce hug. "Try and get some rest. If you need us let us know." She stepped back. "Love you little sister."

Ilana's shoulders slumped in resignation. "Love you too." She had managed to snap at her mom and her sister. Neither one of them snapped back. They wanted to help, and she wished they could. Her apartment. That's all she wanted. Everything else could wait.

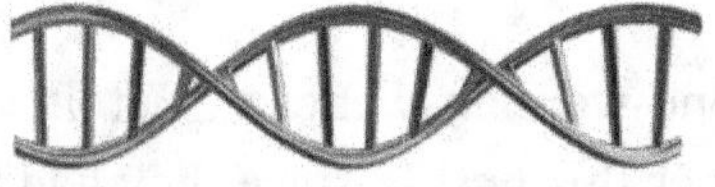

Roark jammed his finger into what essentially worked as a door for Ethan and Ilana's unit. He scrubbed his hand over his face. Talisa had already warned him that their daughter was on edge. Rightfully so. Hell, most of his kids were. James had called him rusty a few times. His son wasn't wrong.

"Charlotte, I told you I'm fine." The hostile glare and clenched jaw on Ilana's face left little to the imagination about how she really felt. Her shoulders relaxed just enough that she no longer looked as if she would attack. "Daddy."

"Hey kiddo." Roark kissed her forehead. "Mind if I come in?"

"Sure. I mean, if you want to." Ilana attempted a non-committal shrug that felt forced.

"I haven't gotten to spend much time with you, really any of your siblings, since we've been back." He slung his arm around her shoulder. "You good with hanging out with your old man for a bit?"

"I am if you are. Don't you have stuff to do?" Ilana led him over to the couch. She tucked her feet underneath herself.

Roark settled on the couch next to her, "There's always stuff to do around here, but you and your siblings are just as important. Neil is going down to help your mom. I just spent some time with James. It's your turn. You've had a rough few days."

Ilana snuggled into his shoulder. "I guess."

"Not much of a guess there, kiddo. You've been disappearing without any explanation and your gifts haven't exactly been in working order." Roark planted a kiss on her temple.

"So." Her one-word answer came out like a petulant child. He hadn't seen her this unsure since they had first gotten their gifts.

"So, it's stressful. It's confusing. Not just for you, but for everyone else around you that wants to help. And it probably feels like your being smothered by it."

Ilana managed a nod.

"Talk to me. Tell me what's going on." He laid his arm on the back of the couch around her. "I know you say you're fine, but I can see that you're not."

His youngest daughter picked at the edge of her fingernail and shrugged instead of answering him.

"Ilana." Roark hooked his finger under her chin and tilted her head up to meet her eyes. "Baby girl, what is going on? Let me help."

"They are trying to kill me." Her answer came out in a whisper, shoulders tense and her eyes squeezed shut.

"Who is trying to kill you?" Roark kept his voice calm and even despite his internal turmoil.

"The Spirits. They are trying to take back what they gave me and kill me in the process." Tears rimmed the edges of her eyes."

"Okay, why do you think that?" He cupped her cheek and thumbed away a tear that escaped. The damn broke. A choked sob escaped from her, and the details spilled out. Phasing out when Inessa tripped over her. Half phasing while waiting for Ethan to take a shower. The dreams. The disappearing. Everything she had been dealing with all punctuated by sobs.

"It's no wonder she's been so torn up." Talisa's voice slipped into his mind.

"Li, this is way beyond my understanding. This is more Chance or Lucas' territory."

"Well, she's not opening up to them. She's opening up to you. You've got this."

"I hope you're right." Who was he kidding? She usually was.

"Of course, I am. I'm your wife." Talisa's chuckle receded to the back of his mind.

"Daddy, I don't want to die." Ilana gripped the front of his shirt."

"Hey…hey…" Roark wrapped her up in his arms and kissed the top of her head. "We aren't going to let that happen. We're going to figure this out. You said you're like a balloon but when you realize your wings aren't out is when you fall to the ground?"

"Mmhmm. And I wake up with broken bones and cuts and bruises." Her tears soaked the front of his shirt.

"What if it's like Ethan said? You have to believe in yourself."

Ilana let out a snotty snort against his chest. "Right. Click my heels three times and I can just fly. Got any pixie dust laying around?"

"There might be some glitter in one of the storage rooms, but I don't think that will help." Roark tilted her head up again to search her eyes. "When was the last time you slept? Remember how impaired Charlotte's powers were when she avoided sleeping for too long?"

The palpable fear that came off of Ilana as she shook her head emphatically worried him. "No. I can't. They'll take it back. They'll kill me."

Roark gripped her shoulders to hold her still. "Easy. I don't believe for a second that they are trying to kill you. Teach you something, yes but not kill you. What if I stayed with you while you nap for a little while?"

"I…I don't know." The woman in front of him regressed to a scared little girl. She looked terrified at the idea.

"I'll be right here. And while you nap, I will pray to the Spirits to give you guidance and knowledge." He pressed his lips to her forehead.

"You'll stay with me?"

"The whole time. I'll be right here and if it looks like you're having a bad dream, I'll wake you up. Deal?" Roark hoped she took him up on the offer. He still hadn't told her about Steele heading towards them soon and how everyone else was getting ready to fight.

Ilana covered a deep yawn that escaped. "I can try. I've been trying to sleep next to Ethan."

"I know I'm no replacement for your husband, but I will do my best." He smiled down at her. "Just try."

Her answer came in the form of a sleepy nod. "K."

Roark scooted down the couch to give her more room to stretch out. He ran his hand along her back. "Love you, Ilana."

"Love you too, Daddy."

"Thank you, Annie. We appreciate the information." Chance looked between the two Johnson women. Both had been put through the wringer the last few weeks. He could only hope that his previous vision would hold true, and they would be planning for another addition to their group.

"Go and try to relax, Annie. We've got this." Abby inclined her head towards him and Inessa. A wave of calm filtered through the room.

"Mom, there's a genocidal maniac on his way to try and kill us. How does relaxing fit into my next few hours? I have to explain to James that I need to be in this fight." Annie shook her head, "Not exactly relaxing."

"Annie, I don't know about that. We just got you back." Abby's eyebrows pinched into a V.

"We all have to do what we can. In my case that means starting with that and bargaining James down to communication with the understanding that if I'm needed topside, I'll be going up there to join the fight." One of Annie's shoulders rose in a shrug.

Inessa's laughter filled the room. "You definitely figured out how to play that game."

"Eh, I wasn't dead that long." Annie leaned in and kissed her mother's cheek. "I'm going to go try your suggestion of relaxing until James is done beating up his father."

Abby squeezed her daughter's hand. "Be alert if you go topside."

"I will, Mom. Love you." Annie squeezed her mother's hand back and walked out of the room.

"Barely back to life a day and already jumping in like she's been here the whole time." Chance rubbed his forehead. "She's got a point. James will be useless if he's worried about her." He spread the area map out on the table. "We have no idea exactly when he's coming or how or from which direction. How the hell are we supposed to plan for that?"

"Breathe Chance." Inessa ran her hand along his back. "Abby hit him again." This time a wave of calm mingled with relaxation.

"Relaxed or not he's right though. Warren isn't up to running communications like he normally would. We've got Annie running that. Inessa is taking charge of those that can't fight with Neil, Tori, and Danny." Abby chewed on her thumbnail. "I'm not thrilled about Kenzie going up there. If anything happens to her, Ariel will kill us."

The door to the conference room slid open. "Why would I kill you?" Ariel walked into the room. "I need to talk to you."

Chance studied the new addition to the room. It had been a year since Ariel had gone anywhere other than the medical area. She looked healthier. "Is something wrong…?" Inessa grabbed his arm and gave a quick shake of her head. She saw something in the woman's aura.

"Steele is on his way."

"We know." Chance nodded slowly. Had Lucas or Kenzie told her that the maniac was enroute?

"Easy now, handsome, grey is not a good color on you." Inessa waived at Ariel, "Hi, I'm Inessa."

"Nice to meet you. Lucas and Kenzie mentioned you joining us." Ariel glanced at Abby. "I also heard you have a daughter. Mazel Tov."

Abby wrapped her arm around Ariel's shoulder and hugged her. "I have missed you, Ariel. So, Lucas and Kenzie mentioned Steele too?"

"No…" Ariel chewed on her bottom lip.

"Okay if they didn't tell you then how did you know?" Chance leaned on the table in front of him. He had a feeling he wasn't going to like the answer. The look on Ariel's face combined with the way Inessa studied her did not bode well.

"Kaliya told me." Ariel switched to wringing her hands together which prompted more assistance from Abby.

"Well, I don't know who that is, but I'm seeing a lot of mixed pinks, greys and reds when you say that name." Inessa continued to study Ariel.

"She…" Ariel inhaled a deep breath and let it out slowly.

"Ariel, whatever it is we're here for you." Chance pushed off the table and pulled Ariel into a hug. "We have missed you so much. Whatever it is, it can't be that bad."

"You say that now. If it involves Steele, it's bad." Her words came out muffled against his chest.

"Once you tell us, we can deal with it." Chance rubbed her back and took a step back to give her some space. Honestly, he had no idea how she would react anymore.

"Like a bandage?" Ariel clutched her hands together.

"Typically, the best way with this group." Abby encouraged her.

"Kaliya is an Exceptional that is with Steele. She's been trained by him. God knows how many other Exceptionals gifts have been grafted on to her DNA. Joe being one of them. The took pieces of him off the battlefield and merged them with her." Tears welled up in Ariel's eyes. When that happened, it reactivated the connection I had with Joe. Well now with Kaliya. We've only spoken a couple of times, but she has some of Joe's memories. She let me know that they received some transmission and they're trying to decrypt it."

"Holy shit." Chance laid his hands on her shoulder. "Ariel, are you okay?" The expressions on Abby and Inessa's faces were both equally aghast.

"I-I don't know." Ariel shrugged. "I really don't. I know it's time I stopped moping around my room though. If that asshole is on his way, I'm going to help."

"We've got communications covered." Abby ran her hand along Ariel's back.

"I'm not staying below. That didn't work out so well for me last time. If I can, I'm going to throw that asshole off a fucking cliff." A low growl rumbled through Ariel's chest.

"I think there's a line. Maybe we'll draw straws. I don't know." Chance dropped a kiss on the top of Ariel's head. "We're just glad to have you back."

Ariel laughed, "Kenzie said the same thing earlier. I can't say I'm ready to come face-to-face with someone who Joe is a part of and fight them, but I'm not going to sit on my ass anymore."

Chance smiled at the women in the room. "Let's go over a few scenarios so we're prepared."

Neil sat in a chair next to one of the tables. He'd come down to help Talisa with the little girl that had been put in a medically induced coma. Lots of variables after she had been removed from one of the stasis pods. Not that he expected to be much help, especially since he couldn't see. "So, she's trying to wake up, but you can't figure out how or why?"

"Stop that." Talisa chastised him.

"Stop what?" Neil could only assume he had been projecting his thoughts to his mother-in-law. The thought had been the truth though. He couldn't see. How did anyone expect him to be a doctor like that? "Ow!" He jerked back as an object hit him in the back of the head. It felt like a rolled-up paper hit him.

"I said stop that. Right now, I need you for your brain. Once we get through this whole current debacle, we will discuss what Charlotte has been working on and how we can help." Talisa's hand came to rest on his arm. "I know there's something I'm missing here. I can't tell why she is waking up."

"I'm confused. Are we trying to keep her asleep still? With Steele on his way, we have to ensure she's protected. Is it better for her to be awake or still in this coma?" Neil wasn't sure there was a right answer to his question. They had no idea what she would be like when she woke up. Would she listen? Would she behave? Would she be terrified of them?

"It's a crapshoot." The uncertainty returned to Talisa's voice.

"You and Abby estimated about an hour, right? At this point if she's going to wake up anyway, perhaps back her off the medication and remove the ventilator. It's the first thing she's going to claw at." At least the typical response for some patients was to claw at anything they could get their hands on. A sixish year old would be terrified waking up in a strange place with people she didn't know.

"We don't honestly know how she's going to react. We know that I worked with her while we were with Steele, but I don't remember anything about that time. I only got brief flashes and they were already in the stasis pods. She might know me. She might be terrified of me." Talisa's feet moving around the room was the only indication she wasn't standing still.

The little bits of shadow and light he could make out didn't aid him in anyway or give him any hint at what Talisa doing. "Did all this start when the alarms went off? She was stable before that right?"

Talisa's voice came from his right. "Abby was down here both times the alarms started going off."

"So more than once. Which ones?"

"All of them. Sometimes all together. Other times alternating. Her vitals were all over the place, too high then too low. Both times they coincided with Ilana disappearing from existence." The edge of concern became clear in Talisa's voice.

"Vitals all over the place and alarms going off when Ilana disappeared from existence. Talisa you're leaving something out. I can hear it in your inflection." Neil knew his mother-in-law well enough to know when she wasn't being completely forthright. Being essentially blind for the better part of a year had also made him pay more attention to the *way* people spoke since he couldn't rely on body language anymore.

"Ilana was drawn down here by a glowing orb. Abby said right before she disappeared, Illy mentioned that the orb has disappeared into the girl, and she was glowing."

"Glowing…" Neil could envision Talisa yanking her ponytail out and putting it back up as she so often did when she pondered a problem just from hearing her hair rustle around her.

"Your other senses have definitely stepped it up a notch. Sorry wasn't trying to pry but the look on your face made me curious. You're right, I was redoing my ponytail. So yes…glowing."

"Like her skin was on fire like a gift type glowing?" More and more this didn't sound like a medical problem at all.

"Kind of in the realm of Spirit orb. At least that's the only thing I can come up with."

"If there's one thing I've learned being married to Charlotte and being around this family is that sometimes it's best not to ask questions. If that's what happened, I would say let her wake up. Back off the medicine. I don't think this is medical." The worst thing they would have to deal with was a scared little girl. He wasn't the best choice for her to see first with the way his face looked. Neil vividly remembered the images Lucas had shown him telepathically. Scaring her with the phantom of the compound not the greatest idea.

"Maybe you're right. We've been looking mainly at the medical aspect. If it's spiritual, then there is nothing we can do to stop it."

"See what happens. We're here if something goes wrong." Neil shrugged but he had no clue if Talisa even looked in his direction.

"True. The timing is just odd with Steele on his way here."

"When is the timing ever optimal? Everything happens as it should. Isn't that what you have always told me?" Neil jerked back. The rolled-up paper hit him again, this time in the shoulder. "Hey!"

"Hey yourself. You don't get to say that to me while you're mentally tearing yourself down. I guess you're what Ariel and Lucas would call a projector." Talisa's hand came to rest on his shoulder. "You are not a monster. Neil, you are a good man. A 'monster' is on his way here."

James pulled the door to the house shut behind him. He spotted her in an instant. Her hair billowed around her with the breeze. She looked peaceful. Spirits, she looked beautiful in the moonlight. Memories from the last time he found her up here like this tugged the corners of his mouth into a smile.

"There you are. I've been looking for you." He set his hands on her shoulders as he kissed the top of her head.

Annie tucked her hair behind her ear and granted him a small smile when she turned to look at him. "I'm sorry I didn't mean to worry you. I just needed some air."

"I'm not surprised. The last time you were topside was…" His voice trailed off. The last time they had been topside together, she had asked him to kill her as a traitor. Then she dropped the bombs from her visions. James straddled the wall next to her to make it easier to pull her against him.

"In my defense, I was having a bad day." Annie snuggled into him and wrapped her arms on top of his. "How was training with your dad?"

"Old man is rusty." Just holding her released the tension in his body.

"Rusty, huh?" Annie shifted to face him. She leaned in and pressed a soft kiss to his lips.

"After a year being stuck with Steele definitely. How did your project go?" The smile on his face shifted to match the frown on her face. "What's wrong?"

"Definitely a trigger. It was buried under so many subroutines that I'm not surprised that no one found it. Me coming here is what set it off."

James studied her quietly. He tucked a lock of hair that the breeze had loosened behind her ear. Just looking at her he could tell that finding the answer hadn't given her any peace. "So, you're struggling with being mad at him."

"You could say that. Me being here is what turned him into a raging asshole that tried to kill me. Anything threatening his connection to me made it worse." Annie's gaze drifted to her lap.

"Hey," James hooked a finger under her chin to make eye contact with her. "If anyone understands getting pissed when their connection to you is threatened it's me. We'll figure it out."

Annie planted a quick kiss on his lips and laid her head on his chest. "There's something else we need to talk about."

"You need to hide your face from me to tell me?" James pulled back just enough to make her look at him. He had a feeling that he wasn't going to like whatever the topic was.

A weak laugh escaped from her. "No, I was just enjoying being able to be close to you."

"You know you can tell me anything, Anne." He smiled back at her. The expression still felt foreign to him.

"Steele."

"Weren't we already taking about him?"

Annie swatted at his arm half-heartedly. "You are such a smartass."

"But ya love me."

"That I do." She leaned in again to kiss him.

This time he didn't let her pull back. His fingers threaded into her hair holding her in the kiss. The soft sigh that escaped from her made him want to take things further. Somehow, he mentally kicked himself enough to pull back. He cleared his throat, "Sorry. Couldn't help myself."

"I wasn't complaining." She cleared her own throat. "Yup, life or death stuff first."

"Right, we need to be responsible." Fuck. Who the hell was he. Instinct told him to take her back to their room to see where that kiss would lead. The madman bearing down on them had other plans for them apparently.

"Steele received the transmission. It *is* encrypted but definitely not up to Dad's normal levels. Didn't take long for me to get through it. It's only going to give us an hour. Maybe two."

"We need to let Chance know." James ran his fingertips along her arm.

Annie shook her head. "I already let them know. He's with my mom planning."

"Okay, but you sounded like we had something more serious to talk about."

"We do." She blew out a breath hesitating.

"What is it, Anne?" James watched as she intertwined her fingers with his.

"I love you, James."

"I love you too, Anne. This feels like a trap." Tension ratcheted up his spine. Now he knew he wouldn't like whatever she had to tell him.

"It's going to be all hands on deck when Steele gets here. Anyone with any type of offensive gift is going to be fighting with everyone else."

Realization struck him the moment the words tumbled from her lips. "No. Anne, no. You can't mean that you're going to be out here fighting." She had already died. Hell, they had just gotten her back. He couldn't lose her to Steele now.

Annie cupped his cheek with her hand. "Pischk. Ehoalan. With the way I can manipulate molecules and computers? Yes, I will be fighting beside you. Okay maybe a little further back than you but I'm going to fight for our home and our life."

James pulled back from her. The thought of something happening to her sent a stabbing pain through his heart. He wanted to, no he *needed* to keep her safe. "Anne please. Don't. I can't survive without you." He cradled her face in his hands. "I just got you back. I can't lose you."

"James…" Annie leaned in and pressed her lips to his. "Okay." She relented. "I'll start out in surveillance from my dad's office but if I'm needed out here. I will come out and help. Deal?"

"I still don't like the thought of you out here fighting, but something tells me it's the best I'm going to get." He pulled her close and nestled her head under his chin. "I can't lose you Anne."

Annie pulled back to meet his eyes with nothing but love and understanding in them. "I can't lose you either, James."

James pulled her close and crushed his lips to hers in a hungry kiss. One hand entwined into her hair while the other ran along her back. When they finally separated, both needing air, he pressed another kiss to her forehead. "How long?"

"Hmm?" Annie's fingers had gripped and twisted his shirt to the point that it felt tight.

"How long do we have until the maniac gets here?" James wanted as much time with her as possible before the fight came to them.

"If I'm going to help run communications I have about an hour before I need to get all the equipment ready for everyone. What did you have in mind?" Annie giggled as his lips trailed along her throat.

"I think you have an idea."

"Mr. Nashuk, I like how you think." Annie swung her legs over the stone wall and stood up. "Lead the way."

"Don't have to tell me twice."

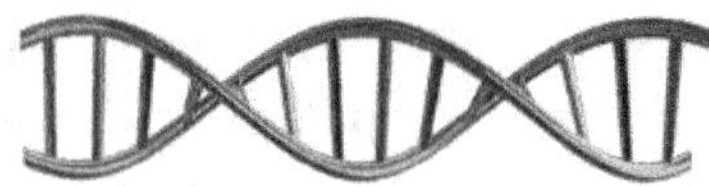

"Alright Kaliya, you just have to lie still while this test runs and then you'll be all set." Taylor adjusted one of the electrodes on her shoulder.

"Thank you, Taylor. Do you think I'll be cleared for the impending fight?" Kaliya stared at the ceiling while the test ran. She had lost track of what this particular test would tell them. The last year and a half of her life had been nothing but experiments and tests. All for a man that called her 'it'.

"I think you'll be fine to join the fight. Don't be nervous." Taylor laid a hand on Kaliya's arm.

"No, Ma'am. I'm not nervous. Just wondering what happens to me after we win this fight." The words came out of her mouth, but she didn't believe them. Something in the back of her mind told her that the Exceptionals were a formidable group. She did worry though. What *would* happen to her if they won? Steele hated those with gifts. Labeled us 'Infected'.

Taylor gave Kaliya's arm a gentle squeeze. "This resistance cell is only the beginning. There are still resistance cells all over the world. We'll need you in the fight for a while to come."

"But what then?" Kaliya asked an honest question. When everything was all said and done. What would the General do with her?

"What do you mean?" Taylor sounded confused.

"If General Steele eliminates the rest of the Infected, will I have any purpose for him?"

"I don't have an answer for that Kaliya. He might not have a use for me either." Taylor winced as she gingerly touched her throat. "We don't know what he'll do. We can only follow his orders as he gives them. Where is all this coming from?" Taylor sat down next to the table Kaliya was lying on.

"Just wondering. That's all. Trying to anticipate what will be expected of me." Kaliya closed her eyes and images of Ariel and others in the resistance flashed through her mind. More of Joe's memories regenerating. At what point would she cease to be herself?

"I try not to think too long term since the General has been known to change his mind. I can tell you when you do attack to hang back. He's going to send in the young soldiers as cannon fodder. Some of the other Infected that experiments were done on too. They'll hold you back with the big guns. You're his secret weapon."

"Let us hope that I perform well for the General then."

"Rest now while the test runs. I'll be right over here if you need anything." Taylor gave her arm a final squeeze.

"You're so conflicted I can feel it from here. Are you okay?" Ariel's voice drifted into Kaliya's mind.

"Nervous. They are running the final tests on me while the message is decrypted." The touch of Ariel's mind in her own brought comfort. Even if it did have to do with Joe's DNA being grafted onto hers. It felt familiar. Like home.

"If it helps, I'm nervous too. I've barely left my quarters since Joe died and I'm jumping straight to the battlefield." An image of Ariel in a mirror filtered into Kaliya's mind. Ariel took sections of hair and braided them into smaller braids before adding them to larger ones to keep her long auburn locks out of the way.

"Ari, no. You cannot go out there. You could be injured or worse." Kaliya let her worry flow through their connection.

"I don't have a choice, Liya. Both Kenzie and I will be up there. Anyone with an offensive gift is going to fight. We have to protect our home."

"Mackenzie as well?! I do not like this. I know we are just getting to know each other but the thought of something happening to any of you upsets me. Will Victoria fight too?" It took every ounce of restraint not to show any outward sign of her internal distress. If Taylor suspected something was off, they would not let her go to the fight. Apparently, that would be the only way she could protect Ariel and the girls.

"No. Tori is going to remain below with the ones that cannot fight or don't have offensive gifts."

"I do not like it. I feel like Joe would not have allowed it." Mentally Kaliya winced at her own words. What right did she have to ask Ariel to stay behind? She had every right to protect her home. The home that Kaliya was preparing to come in and destroy.

"You're right. Joe would have fought Kenzie and I on it. He would do anything to ensure we were safe." Tears and sadness tinged Ariel's mental voice.

"Yet you will still put yourselves in danger now. I do not understand. The Infected…"

"No. Liya, stop. You are not infected. I don't know why Steele thinks of it that way unless he's jealous that he didn't get powers. You are not one of his Infected. You are an Exceptional." Ariel's firm stance came through in her voice.

"The General calls me 'it'. Does not use my name." Sorrow and grief went back to Ariel from Kaliya.

"Well, he's a fucking idiot." Ariel projected the image of herself in the mirror through their connection. *"Your name is Kaliya. You are an Exceptional. You are not infected. You are amazing. Yes, they did things to you, but it's because they did that we have this connection. It's a gift."*

"Thank you for saying that, Ariel. I have been struggling with my role in all of this. I wanted the General to be happy with me."

"Most of the people I know did. Look where that got them? He used Talisa to release the original virus that made us Exceptionals. He kidnapped her and her husband while torturing them and trying to get them to recreate our gifts. I'm beginning to think he's envious."

A laugh escaped from Kaliya. She coughed to cover it up with Taylor. *"I did not realize how much I needed to laugh. Thank you, Ari."*

"I'll see you soon, Liya. Be careful."

Mackenzie counted each item as it floated up onto the high shelf. Since getting a handle on her gift she tended to use it for mundane things like this. Soon Steele would be here, and she would be using it against other human beings. It didn't matter if they were Exceptional or not. It still felt wrong.

"Mackenzie?" Lucas' voice caught her attention.

"Back here." She called out to her husband but continued getting the supplies ready for those that would be staying below. Like her sister.

Lucas stole a quick kiss, "How are the supplies looking down here?"

"Not too bad. We're going to need to make a run soon though. Starting to run low on a few things." A run. Who was she kidding? A run consisted of trying to buy things the legal way and when that didn't work, they stole what they needed. Thankfully they had a few Exceptionals with horticultural gifts.

"I wish you would stay below with your sister." Lucas smoothed her hair out of her face.

"I wish you were staying below too. I have offensive gifts, so I'll fight. Both you and James made sure we were all prepared for this." Mackenzie stopped long enough to give him a quick peck. "My mother…that's another story. She's barely left her room in a year and she's going out there to fight. Let's not forget that she could come face-to-face with a woman that now has some of my Dad's DNA."

"We would worry more if things were simple. Nothing worthwhile is ever easy."

"Then everything we do is extremely worthwhile husband. We tend to take the path less traveled." Mackenzie wrapped her arms around Lucas' waist. The cans had settled onto the shelf.

Lucas pulled her close. "You are always worth it, Mackenzie. You worry for more than just your mother."

"Tori. She's been spending a lot of time with Chaz. It doesn't sound like he'll hurt her, but just the little bit I heard about what Steele put him through worries me." It worried her a lot. Some described him as more animal than man. Caiman had been the only one that could help him until suddenly her sister got him to sleep.

"Caiman would put a stop to it if she thought Tori was in danger. Danny would intervene as well. From what I've heard, Chaz finds it very hard to get to sleep and Tori has actually been able to get him to rest." Lucas shrugged, "They are drawn to each other."

Mackenzie smiled at her husband. "I can understand that. As long as she's safe. I am glad she'll be below though. She can fight, but I don't think being a mimic will help her with this fight."

"I convinced her that I needed her to ensure the safety of everyone that would be down below."

"So, you played to her ego. I love my little sister, but she's a stubborn one." She grabbed a few of the boxes with her hands instead of her gifts and aligned them on the shelf. "What about you? Most of your family will be up there."

"Ilana and I are the only ones without some form of healing. I worry for Caiman. If she comes face-to-face with Steele she may act rashly. Danny is staying below so he will not be able to temper her decisions." Lucas lifted a few boxes of his own to put on the shelf next to hers.

"How's Illy doing? I know the Houdini act has got to be wearing on her." She stopped to sit on a stack of boxes. Organizing this storage room only served as a way to keep her busy until it was time to go and fight. Everyone else had something to do in the meantime. Planning. Getting communications ready. Mackenzie was counting how many cans of black beans they had left.

"From what my mother tells me, she's struggling. My father got her to nap at least. She has not been sleeping."

"We all know how that affected Charlotte when she wasn't sleeping."

"Precisely. She has things to learn but she has closed herself off from hearing it. Until she stops that, this will continue. I don't know how to help her." Lucas's shoulder's slumped in defeat. Not something she saw often.

Mackenzie shot back to her feet in front of her husband. She cupped his cheek with her hand, "Hey, none of that. You are helping her the best you can. Illy has to be willing to learn those lessons. You can't force it on her. She'll learn when she needs to."

Lucas looked at his wife, pleased. "Sometimes I need you to remind me that I am doing what I can."

"That's my job as your wife. In fact, something tells me that once Ilana gets through this, she's going to need one of your herbal concoctions to help her process it all. If she's going to keep disappearing like this, then she has a lot to learn and it's important." Mackenzie pressed her lips to his in a soft kiss.

"You, my wife, are beautiful, and brilliant." Lucas returned her kiss then pressed his lips to her forehead.

"I just know from our experiences that sometimes you just have to listen. Typically, when you want to the least. We learned that the hard way." She shuddered at the thought of everything they went through to be together. Not listening almost cost them their relationship.

"Yes, we did. But we made it through." Lucas smiled down at her. "I'll go work on that concoction, as you called it."

Laughter bubbled up in her, "I don't know what else to call it. The bigger the problem, the more herbs you end up using." She planted a kiss on his lips. "Go work on that. I'll see you in a bit."

"Yes ma'am. I know when to listen to my wife. I love you, Mackenzie."

"Love you too, Lucas."

Ilana floated high above the neighborhood that camouflaged the compound beneath it. The sun and the air on her face felt amazing. It felt freeing. She reached for the clouds as she always did, despite knowing the impossibility of actually touching them.

Ready to continue on her journey she attempted to flap her wings. Realization slammed into her that once again they were missing.

182

"Oh God. Not again." Tears sprung from her eyes along with the panic that welled up inside of her.

The rope wrapped loose around her ankle gave a gentle tug. She bent over in what felt like a futile attempt to free herself. Maybe the trial was to free herself from the rope. With a yell of relief, she pulled the rope free and held it in her hand. Ilana looked around not sure what she expected to happen.

"That feels too easy."

It *was* too easy. The rope snaked around her wrist in an elaborate knot. With a hard tug she began to plummet headfirst towards the ground. Oh God she really was going to die. They were going to kill her.

You fight what you are.

Her breath rushed out of her body as the ground came rushing up towards her. Ilana brought her arms up as if they would cushion a fall from several hundred feet in the air. Ethan. She never got to apologize to Ethan. Here she was about to die and the last thing she said to her husband was in anger. Her husband. Her sister. Her mother. She had been horrible to all of them.

The impact sent waves of searing pain through her body. The remaining air in her lungs hissed out. All-encompassing pain. Then nothing. This was it. The end.

The world faded away. The trees, the ground, the grass. It all disappeared. Ilana laid face down on a cold flat surface. Did her family already find her and take her to the lab?

"Jesus Fuck! Ilana! Baby, no!" Roark's voice jarred her from her throughs.

Ilana pushed against the cold flat surface to stand up. Instead of standing up she tumbled to the ground. She looked up only to realize she had been lying on the ceiling. "Daddy?"

Roark showed no reaction to her voice. "I don't know, Li. She was sleeping and her body just started convulsing. Her skin it's changing color."

With her head tilted to the side she approached the body on the couch. Ilana knew from the way her father spoke it was also a mental conversation with her mother. Her body. Transforming. Her father was about to see her Skinwalker appearance. Only Ethan had ever seen it. She had always been extremely careful.

Roark gripped her shoulders and shook her, tears streaming down his face. "Wake up, baby. Come back to us please."

Ilana reached out to touch herself. Her hand slipped through as if she wasn't even there. "That's new. Am I still dreaming?"

"What the fuck?" Roark jumped back from the couch. Brown weblike fibers started to wrap themselves around the legs of her body. They continued up until she was completely covered. "I don't know Li. She looks like a fucking mummy. Nothing in our medical training covered this."

Roark wasn't wrong. None of them had ever seen anything like this. She didn't remember ever reading anything like this in any of the texts they had been able to salvage. What the fuck indeed. The more the weblike material covered her body it looked more like a cocoon than mummification. Was there even a word for what she was watching or what was happening to her?'

Giddy laughter bubbled up inside her. This was the end. It was over. She was dead. Relief flooded through her. No more fighting. No more cryptic messages. Free. Free of feeling inadequate.

A pang of regret and sadness stuck. Watching her father morn and freak out over her dead and changing body felt wrong. Ilana wanted to comfort him.

"You are not dead child. Impatient like your mother, but not dead."

Ilana startled and spun around. "Uma!" Her grandmother stood before her. "If I'm not dead then what's happening to me?" The quick hint of disappointment felt odd and foreign to her.

"You would not listen before so now you will be made to listen. You cannot save your people if you do not."

"Grandmother, that makes no sense. Why not just talk to me instead of literally breaking me?"

Her grandmother stepped forward and smoothed the hair back from Ilana's face. "My dear child, you closed yourself off from us. You did not believe. You gave up. When you fight it, there are consequences."

Ilana leaned into her grandmother's hand. It felt so real as they stood there. "Ethan said I needed to believe in myself."

"Your Ethan is wise in saying that. You limit yourself." Her other hand came up to cup the other side of Ilana's face.

"Wait. Is it that easy? Like he said just believe I can fly?"

"Oh no." The old woman chuckled. "But it is part of it. You carry too much guilt. People died but it was not your doing. You saved who you could."

Tears caught in Ilana's throat. "Uma, so many people died because I couldn't stop it."

"Many people died all over the world. Were they your fault as well?" Uma shook her head, "No. You cannot bear the weight of the world child. You only have two shoulders."

"But our people. You and Grandfather." A sob threatened to choke her.

"Do I look in ill health?" Uma turned on from side-to-side. She cast a smile at Ilana's slightly sniffly giggle that escaped. "I am on a different plane of existence. We still watch over you."

"What do I do now though?" Ilana gestured towards her father still freaking out over her now fully cocooned body.

"Now, my child. You learn."

Talisa checked the little girl's vitals for what felt like the millionth time. Each time they had steadily improved. There was no doubt she would be awake soon. She rubbed her hands along her forehead. What could happen after that is what worried her.

Roark was dealing with the new development with Ilana. If you could call freaking out dealing with it. Thankfully, Lucas was on his way to assist his father. Nothing like her husband described had ever happened before. A cocoon. What the hell would cause a cocoon? This was one of the few times she wished for the ability to be in two places at once.

A small groan escaped from the little girl's parted lips. Talisa checked the pad over and everything remained stable. "Easy. Take it slow."

Her little lashes fluttered to reveal two beautiful deep brown eyes. They looked like two dark stones smoothed by the rush of the river. Wise and aware. A few slow blinks and she focused on Talisa's face. "Grams!"

Talisa's face went slack. Not the reaction she expected. Who are you? Sure. Where am I? Absolutely. A name indicating the girl knew her affectionately? Completely unexpected. She shook it off and smiled down at her. "You know who I am?"

The girl nodded with gusto. "You're my Grams. Can I sit up? I feel weird flat on my back."

"Uh, sure." Talisa moved to adjust the bed. Each clack of the metal moved the bed further into a semi-sitting position. "Let me get you some water. You've got to be thirsty."

"Thank you." The little girl took the glass of water from Talisa and took several long sips.

"So, you know who I am. What is your name?" This day couldn't get any more insane. Who was she kidding? The barbarian would be at the gates soon. She sat on the stool she had slid up next to the bed.

"I'm Orenda. I'm six." Her giggle filled the lab.

"Orenda is it?" A smile spread across her face. There would be growing pains with the family, but it would be another thing they would deal with. "Do you know where you are?"

The girl's shoulders rose in a shrug. "A lab?"

"We're in our hiding place away from the bad man." It had been a long time since Talisa had to explain things to a small child. All of their children grew up so fast. Literally.

"Our family is here though."

"Do you know who your family is?" Talisa bit the inside of her cheek unsure of what kind of answer she would get.

Orenda held up her hands to count on her fingers. "I have lots, so I need these. Um…" She held one finger to her lips and looked up towards the ceiling. "Aunt Charlotte and Uncle Neil, Momma and Danny." She shook her head. "She's not ready. Uncle James and Aunt Annie, Aunt Kat, Uncle Lucas and Aunt

Kenzie, and Aunt Illy and Uncle Ethan. She's busy right now though."

Talisa's mouth hung open slack jawed. Orenda had a grasp on more than she ever expected. "O-kay. That's very good."

"I can count to one hundred too." Her granddaughter nodded with a grin.

"That's wonderful. Maybe you can show Danny in a little while. There are some things going on and we're going to need to move you to where you'll be safe." This would be great if Danny's head didn't explode. Here's your stepdaughter. She just woke up. Keep an eye on her while we go fight the monster.

The questioning tilt to her granddaughter's head was almost comical. "Danny doesn't know how to count?"

Talisa chuckled, "He does. I just meant you can show him how you can. I'm sure he'll like that. You also have your grandfather.

"Gramps is with Illy. Is Lucas gonna help him calm down? Freaking out isn't gonna help her." Orenda looked up at Talisa as if she had asked the most innocent question in the world.

"What do you know about what's going on with Ilana?" Why not ask the six-year-old about the cocoon? Makes sense. Spirits, she needed a drink.

Orenda made a face as she shook her head, "Illy's not listening." Her arms came up in an 'I don't know' gesture. "They keep trying, but she's blocking them out. She won't wake up until she listens. They tried a few times, but she kept ignoring them. She carries too much."

"So once Ilana listens, she'll come out of the cocoon?"

"I think it's more like a chrisamis." Orenda grinned.

"Do you mean a chrysalis?" Talisa straightened the girl's slightly disheveled hair.

"Yeah that." She bounced excitedly. "Illy is more like a butterfly. She does turn brown though so maybe it's more like a moth. Butterflies are prettier though."

"You seem to know a lot about them." All this conversation did was add to her questions. How did Orenda know about any of this? They still didn't know how long she had been in stasis. Or what her life was like before she was put in stasis.

"Uma taught me."

Blink. That's all Talisa could do. Her granddaughter just told her that Talisa's own mother taught her about butterflies and moths. Uma was the Lenape name for grandmother, which is what the kids called her before she died.

"Now you're not listening, Grams." The six-year-old smirked at her.

"No, I guess I'm not. I need to do better. Why don't we find you something to eat and get you to Danny, hmm? Grams is going to need to help deal with the bad man soon." Talisa held her arms out to pick Orenda up.

The little girl scrambled across the bed into Talisa's arms. She grabbed either side of Talisa's face. "Try and listen while we're getting me food. It will help. I promise."

A grandchild connected to the Spirits. Her parents would have been ecstatic. Chance would tease her endlessly. Talisa gave Orenda a peck on the temple "I will do my best to listen. And when we get through all of this you can meet the rest of the family."

General Steele kicked a trash can out of the way that had the audacity to move into his path as he paced his office. They should have had the location by now. It shouldn't take this long. Then again, he didn't have the same talent working for him as he did in the past.

Everything would have been so much easier if the virus had worked as intended. The buzz of the intercom on his desk interrupted his thoughts. He jammed his finger into it. "What?"

"We have it sir. The location." The voice crackled through the intercom.

His prayers answered. He could wipe out the resistance and work on getting rid of the remaining Infected as they found them. All according to his plan.

"Sir?"

"Yes. Yes. Very good I'm on my way." Steele straightened out his uniform on his way to see the technician. "Soon. All of them would be gone. Shame to lose some of their minds though. Brilliant. But they have to go. All of them have to go. They need to be eradicated."

The technician stood up when Steele entered the room. A clipboard shook in his hand. "Sir we've located them in a remote area near Glasgow, Montana. Satellite surveillance doesn't show much activity on the surface, but they could be masking it somehow."

"Excellent work. Excellent work. We need to rally the troops. It's time to wipe them from the earth." Steele clapped the man on the shoulder.

"Y-yes sir." The technician looked mortified.

"It's time." Steele turned on one foot and strode out the door at a quick pace. "Taylor. It's time." He yelled down the hallway towards Taylor's lab. "Did you hear me? They've been found. It's time to put your little experiment to the test."

Taylor looked up from the microscope she'd been peering into. "General?"

"Good. You're here. Get it ready. It's time. We're leaving as soon as all the troops are mustered." A wide grin spread on his face. This was his dream come true. He couldn't have Talisa so he would wipe out her and her entire family. Even his scheming princess. That family had cost him more than he could stomach. After they escaped, some even had the audacity to question his leadership.

"You have the location?" The skepticism on Taylor's face needled him to no end.

"I told you I would. We have it and we're going to move in. They are in Montana of all places. Is *it* ready?" He inclined his head towards Kaliya. Why on earth Taylor thought to give it a name was beyond him. It was a tool. It was disposable. If it helped him win great. If it perished, so be it.

"I am ready to fight, General." The monster he had created stood up, towering over the man.

"Good. Good. Let's go. We have much to discuss. I want to ensure the primary targets are taken out first." Steele hated being in the same room as it. That thing. Bad enough it had been Infected but the experiments made it look like an abomination.

"Remember what we talked about, Kaliya." Taylor squeezed Kaliya's arm.

"Of course, Taylor." Kaliya bowed to the other woman.

"And what are you filling its head with Taylor? What special information could you have that could help?" Steele laughed at the thought that Taylor would have anything useful to add to its training.

"Taylor went over the powers of the Infected we will be facing General. She wanted to make sure I was prepared for the fight to come." The way Kaliya smiled at him unnerved him.

"Ah good. That will help cut down on the briefing time. Let's get going then." Steele turned without another word to head to the main area of their compound. He tried to ignore the creature that walked with him. It was a necessary evil. You had to fight fire with fire.

A soldier ran up to the pair and saluted Steele. "General sir. The men are gathered. Ready to deploy when you are."

"Excellent. Join your platoon soldier. I'm going to address everyone." Steele glanced up at Kaliya. "Go get into the first chopper."

"Yes, General." Kaliya bowed to him and went to board.

Steele stepped up to the podium and grinned at the sight before him. All these soldiers under his command. His control. They were about to help him accomplish something incredible. Wiping out the main resistance of the Infected and all the evidence with them that he had released the virus to begin with.

"We are about to embark on a historic journey." Steele grinned down at them as they cheered. "The location we've been waiting for is in our grasp. We're going to use it to eliminate the leadership of the Infected Resistance. No longer will they terrorize us. No longer will they destroy our cities. Our monuments. Our country." A cacophony of cheers and yells erupted from below.

"As your leader I promise you, we will return this country to the one we deserve. One clean and clear of the Infected. Where you don't have to worry if your neighbor is secretly Infected with the disgusting virus." They bought it all. Every word that came out of his mouth, they believed. It was amazing to see how much like lemmings they really were.

"Load up. We leave now to eradicate them from the world." Steele grinned down at the group celebrating below. He wondered if they realized that a good number of them would not come home from this. Yes, the Infected needed to go, but some of them had impressive skills and they would take out a good portion of his soldiers.

A necessary evil though. There was always loss in war. Today the Infected would lose.

22

"Do you think he'll help, Abby?" Chance made his way down to the containment area. Despite everything that had happened with Warren, if he could help, they could definitely use him.

"I think he will. He is distraught over how he acted and everything that he did. I'm just not sure how Annie is going to do with them working together." Abby stepped into the containment area just ahead of him.

Chance stopped her just inside the door. He took her shoulders in his hands. "I know we need the help but if you detect the slightest bit off in his emotions then we can't let him out of there right now. We won't be able to risk it."

"I don't think it will be a problem. He'll want to be in his office watching over things. Especially if Ethan and I are going to be in the thick of it." Abby held her hand up as if it would stop his protest.

"Abby, are you sure? I know we said all hands on deck, but no one would fault you for staying down here and helping." Chance knew she had the same training as the rest of them did.

James had made sure anyone with a gift that had the capability of being used in an offensive manner knew how to use it.

Abby shook her head, "You aren't talking me out of it. Ariel and I are going to pair up. Using my gifts for something else other than calming people down and boiling my own tea faster will be a nice change of pace."

"Taking some bargaining lessons from your daughter perhaps?" Chance chuckled at how similar the Johnson women were.

"Who says she didn't learn that from me?" She inclined her head towards Warren's cell. "Come on we need to get this taken care of."

"Abby? Chance?" Warren looked slightly less disheveled but still distressed.

"Hey Warren. I wish I had more time but we're kind of short on it. Annie checked out your arm and found the trigger virus. She also double checked the encryption on the message you sent out." This whole situation sucked. If the proverbial dragon wasn't at their gates, they would have done more to ensure Warren had been taken care of.

Warren placed his hand on the glass in front of Abby. She reciprocated on their side. "How much time is there?"

"Annie thinks about an hour, hour and a half maybe, if we're lucky. She offered to handle communications, but she could probably use your help if you are feeling up to it. We understand if you aren't though." Abby offered her husband a sad smile.

"We've got a group getting the women and children down to the secure area and you are welcome to go with them if you want." Chance folded his arms across his chest. In the past Abby would stay behind just because of her medical training. He didn't agree with her going out there this time. Fortunately, he learned over the years not to argue with the ranking women in their group. It never ended well.

"I don't know, Chance. Not like I don't deserve to be in here. With Annie and Abby there, will you need my help?" Warren leaned against the glass to stay upright.

"I'm going to be on the surface with Ethan." Abby placed her other hand on their side of the barrier over Warren's heart. "You would be with Annie."

Warren reared back from the barrier. His eyes looked crazed. Not exactly a good sign. "Chance, how can you even think about letting her go up there?"

A wave of calm filled the space. Thank the Spirits for Abby's gifts. The crazed look in Warren's eyes receded back to concern. "I'm letting her go up there just like I'm letting Charlotte or Kenzie or Ariel. I don't like it. We don't have a choice. Annie wanted to go up there too, but James got her to see we need the help with Communications."

Abby straightened up but didn't remove her hand from the barrier. "I need to go out there and do what I can. That man tried to destroy our family."

"I'll help. Whatever you need me to do. If I help Annie, I can help keep an eye on everyone." Warren slumped against the barrier.

"Chance, do I have enough time to take him back to our unit for a shower and some fresh clothes?" Abby looked up at him expectantly.

"Yeah, I think there's time for that. Ariel's going to let us know when she hears from her source." Chance didn't waste any time opening the cell to help Warren over to Abby.

"Wait, Ariel is up and about?" Warren looked between them confused.

"Almost like old times. She was in the conference room with us helping to plan." Abby moved to her husband's side to assist him.

"Is Annie going to be okay with me there?" Warren glanced over at Chance. Most of the man's effort went into staying upright. The loss of a limb was enough to throw anyone's balance off.

"I believe it will be fine. Let her take the lead and you two can go from there." Chance hit the button to open the door back to the main hallway.

"Talisa and Roark just brought her back and I had to go and bring Steele right to our door." Warren shook his head.

Chance laid his hand on Warren's remaining arm. "If anyone understands being manipulated by that maniac, it's Annie."

"She feels just as guilty as you do with all of this. Annie feels responsible since her showing up is what triggered all of this." Abby ran her hand along her husband's back.

The trio stopped in front of Abby and Warren's unit. Chance plugged in the code so their door would open. "You two get cleaned up and comfortable. We need to meet Annie in about forty-five minutes."

"We'll see you there, Chance." Abby cast a small smile over her shoulder.

"Thanks man. We'll see you there." Warren struggled into their apartment with Abby's help but didn't ask for any additional assistance.

Chance waited until the door slid shut. He let his head fall back to stare at the ceiling. "Spirits, please help us."

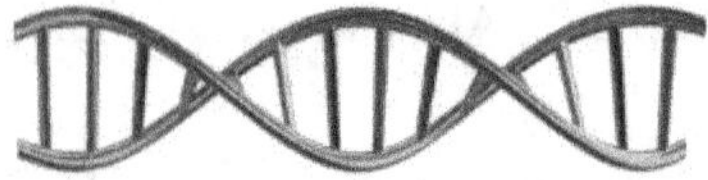

Lucas sprinted down the hallway from his workroom. *"I'm on my way, mother."* The panic in his mother's mental voice let him know how serious the situation was. Ilana in a cocoon? It didn't make any sense. Then again, what Ilana had been experiencing was completely new territory.

"Thank you, Lucas. Keep me posted." Talisa's voice faded out. She had her hands full with the little girl.

"Ilana, please. Come back." Roark knelt next to the cocoon on the couch. His hands hovered just above it as if afraid to touch it.

"Dad." Lucas entered the room and looked around. Nothing felt out of the ordinary or out of place. Well, not nothing. The human sized cocoon on the couch wasn't exactly part of the normal decor.

"Lucas." Roark shot to his feet. "What is going on? You're sister. She was napping. Getting some actual sleep and then suddenly, she started convulsing. Then this web thing surrounded her. Is she still alive? I can't even see if she's breathing."

Ilana being in the cocoon was a worry and a priority, but first he needed to calm his father down. He rarely lost his composure like this. With everything his parents had been through it was understandable though. "Dad, I need you to stop for a moment and breathe."

"How the hell am I supposed to breathe? I was holding her when this happened. Nothing in my medical training explains any of this." Roark paced the length of the couch raking his hands through his hair.

Lucas pursed his lips and watched his father go back and forth. He closed his eyes and inhaled slowly. When he opened his eyes a small wave of water doused his father. The man sputtered and swiped at his face to clear the liquid from his eyes. "Breathe."

Roark glared back at his son. "What the hell was that for?"

"You were near hysterical. I understand this is not something we have dealt with before. We need to approach it with a clear head." Lucas concentrated and one-by-one all the extra water molecules he had thrown at his father we pulled out of his clothing and away from his skin until Roark was once again dry.

"How did you do that?"

"Concentration. We can discuss that at length later." Lucas approached the cocoon and laid his hand on it.

"Careful." Roark snapped.

"I do not believe that touching it will hurt Ilana." A deep breath in and out as Lucas' eyes fell shut. He concentrated on his sister and the Spirits. An image of Ilana standing there with their Uma filtered into his mind. The older woman smoothed back Ilana's hair with a gentle yet wise smile.

"Anything?" Roark's impatient voice boomed behind him.

"Mother is right. You do get impatient when one of us is in danger." Lucas stood up to face his father. "She is learning from the Spirits. Ilana will emerge when she is ready."

"So, you're telling me our family's timing is perfect as always." Roark crossed his arms across his chest.

"More or less." Lucas nodded. "Ilana will emerge once her lessons are completed."

"Maniac on his way to kill us and your sister picked now to go to school, so to speak." Roark sighed.

Lucas chuckled, "You could say that. I believe they picked for her since she would not listen before this. She will be there when she is needed."

"I'm sorry, son. I'm just worried. I know we said all hands on deck and you and your brother and sisters can take care of yourselves, but Steele is insane. Unhinged."

"We know. I do not like that Mackenzie will be fighting either, but I understand her reasons for wanting to be out there." Lucas knew both he and James made sure all the women had been trained properly but the thought of something happening to his wife worried him.

"Lucas…Roark…is Ilana secure? We need to meet in the conference room now." Talisa's voice slammed into both of their brains.

"Ilana is safe mother. She is with the Spirits." Lucas glanced at his father and inclined his head towards the door. "We should go now. No harm will come to Ilana like this. She is protected."

"We're on our way, Li." Roark laid his hand on the cocoon and stared at it for a moment. "You've got this, baby girl."

The two men strode down the hallway towards the conference room. Lucas glanced at the stoic expression on his father's face. "I know you worry about us. We worry about you too. You and mother only just returned to us. We have not had enough time with you."

"There's no way your mother and I want to leave you all again, son. We were gone too long and missed too much. I worry about all of you being out there together."

"We worry for that as well. I might have been able to talk Mackenzie into staying below as she had in the past if Ariel was not planning on fighting topside. While I do not like it, we cannot force anyone *not* to fight." Lucas knew several of the couples had the same conversation. With the exception of Danny and Elan. His gift was more useful close up.

"You're right there. I think we're all worried about Ariel going out there. She hasn't been active since Joe died." Roark stopped and turned towards Lucas. "I know you said concentration, but how did you pull that wave out of thin air? I'm still a little rusty with this new gift. I was able to control water, with considerable effort when we were escaping from Steele, but it was rushing in at us."

Lucas smiled at his father. "You will learn and get stronger with it. You need to remember that there is water in everything. The air, the plants, and people are about sixty percent water."

"You pulled that water literally out of the air?"

"And I put it back after I had your attention." Lucas clapped his father on the shoulder. "I am sure you will be inventive with it on the battlefield, but once this crisis has passed, I can show you a few more tricks."

"Spirits willing, we will come through this unscathed."

Chance stood at one end of the conference table surveying the room. There hadn't been this many people in this space since they had first decided to move their group underground.

Talisa stood next to him, reaching for Roark's hand the moment he and Lucas entered the room.

"I wish I had more details about what we are about to face. The most important one is that Steele is on his way. We don't know from where or how long it will take for him to get here. We do know he has been experimenting on Exceptionals by playing with DNA." Chance nodded in Annie's direction. He prayed to the Spirits that Warren didn't take any offence to his daughter taking point.

Annie for her part didn't falter or flinch away from the responsibility. She opened several cases on the table. "Communications devices are good to go. There's one here for everyone, including those taking point down below with the civilians. Dad and I are working on a back-hack to try and gain access to a few satellite feeds to give us a better visual maybe find a back channel into their communications." She reached down and squeezed Warren's shoulder.

"Good. Keep us up to date. Kenzie how are the supplies looking downstairs?" Chance rubbed the back of his neck in an effort to relieve the growing tension. The last large-scale battle had been a year ago and they lost some good people.

"We're good for now, Chance. Few weeks' worth of canned goods." Mackenzie leaned against Lucas.

"Thank you, Kenzie. We're really in a waiting game now. Everyone needs to be careful out there. There are several of you I would prefer stayed below." He shot a pointed look in Charlotte's direction. His daughter just smirked back at him. "But I understand why you want to be up there."

"I'm going to stay below, Chance." Abby sat next to Warren holding his one remaining hand. "We need at least one medically trained person down here in case of injuries."

"Thank you, Abby. We appreciate—"

"What the fuck?!" Ariel interrupted any other discussion. The woman stood up, eyes wide.

"Mom?" Mackenzie shot to her mother's side.

"Ariel?" Chance stepped around the table keeping, his movements slow as not to startle the woman. She hadn't been out of her room much in the last year so he wasn't sure what would set her off.

Ariel waived her hand, dismissing the people converging on her. "Sorry…sorry. Didn't mean to startle everyone. Steele just left. Thirty to forty-five minutes out."

"Your source?" Chance asked hesitantly. A few people knew the special circumstances, but not everyone.

"Sure. My source." The redhead rolled her eyes at him, "Everyone is going to find out eventually, Chance." She scanned the room. "Steele grafted Joe's DNA onto someone else and now I'm connected to a woman named Kaliya. She's been feeding me information."

"Can we trust this person?" Elan piped up from her spot on the side of the room.

"Remains to be seen. It feels like I can, but we'll see." Ariel shrugged.

Chance scrubbed his hands over his face, "Can we assume your 'what the fuck' had to do with more than him being on his way?" Spirits, he loved this group but if he didn't control the conversation an argument would ensue, and someone usually ended up insulted in the end.

"Yeah, that. The first wave is going to be kids basically. Young soldiers and Exceptionals to be used as cannon fodder. Then he'll send in the big guns." Ariel gripped the chair in front of her.

"That's not new." Elan shrugged, picking at one of her fingernails. "That's pretty standard for him."

"He did that in the last big one we were in too." James added from his spot behind Annie.

"Any Exceptionals are expendable to him." Roark stood behind Talisa and rubbed her shoulders.

"We already know he's insane so this shouldn't surprise anyone." Talisa added leaning back against Roark.

Chance scanned the room again to take a pulse check on everyone. "Now we have a timeframe. Try and be non-lethal, if possible." He held his hand up against the protests he knew were about to come. "I know. Easier said than done. There's a pit past the graveyard and the stream. It's deep enough that if you happen to drop a soldier in there, they won't be able to climb out of it immediately. James, anything to add?"

"Since we weren't sure which direction they were coming in from, there are traps and smaller pits fanning out into the woods. We tried to leave the main neighborhood intact. The barn with the plane is locked up as best we can but try and draw any fighting away from there and towards the woods." James bounced on the balls of his feet. The man was itching for a fight. "We're planning on staying hidden as long as possible to surprise them. We know this area. They don't."

Chance could tell just by looking at them they were all ready to get out there and fight. Hell, he was too. The years running and hiding had taken its toll on all of them. "James is right. We've been living here long enough that we know this area well. Use that to our advantage. No one is still topside in the houses; everyone has been moved below. I know I don't have to say this but be smart in this fight. Be careful and have each other's backs and if you need to fall back…do it."

Most of the group nodded or verbalized agreement with his statement. A few grumbled, but he knew they would do what was necessary.

"Spirits be with you all."

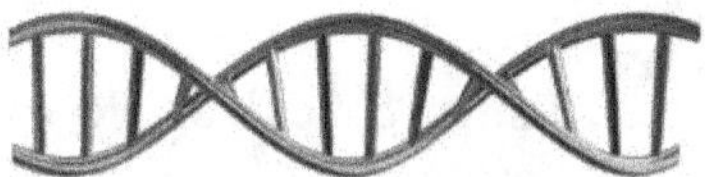

Annie pushed Warren's wheelchair down the hallway towards his office at a fast clip. They needed to make sure that communications stayed up and active during the fight. Her mother walked on one side of her and James on the other. "I fixed a few of the drones I found in the office, but it isn't enough for full coverage. We still have a lot of blind spots."

"Annie, you did what you could in the time you had." A wave of calm came with Abby's statement.

"I know Mom, but I still don't like it. Too many variables." Annie pushed Warren into the office and set him up in his usual spot at his desk. There would be too much pacing to be tied to a chair. Not that either of them actually had to look at the monitors to see the information being displayed. "This good, Dad?"

Warren laid his remaining hand on top of hers. "It's fine Annie. Thank you."

"We'll work with what we've got, Anne. It's going to be fine." James kissed her forehead.

"Be careful." Annie wrapped her arms around James. She knew he could take care of himself, but they hadn't had enough time together.

"I'm always careful." The sexy grin she'd come to love quite quickly tugged at the corners of his mouth.

A coughed laugh escaped from her father behind her. "Some of us know better, James."

"Oh, I'm not jeopardizing this." James pulled Annie's hips towards his.

"Hey now. We're right here." A genuine laugh escaped from Warren.

"Sorry, Cyber." James chuckled. He planted a kiss on Annie's lips. "I promise I'll be careful."

Annie returned the kiss holding on to him tighter. "Thank you. Who's with you?"

"Chance, Charlotte, and Ethan. I'll watch out for them too." James ran his hand along Annie's back.

"Hey sis, you seen…" Ethan stuck his head in the door. "Never mind. Should have known."

"Soon as Chance and Charlotte join us, we'll head up." James didn't let go of Annie either.

Finally, her family together in one place and instead of celebrating they were getting ready to fight a maniac. Somehow in her short actual life this felt normal. "Be careful Ethan."

"I will be, Little Bit." Ethan leaned in and hugged Abby. "I'll be fine Mom."

"You all keep saying that, but we know what can happen out there." Abby fussed over Ethan.

"Mom's right." Annie leaned into James. "Steele is unhinged and he's not fighting with just soldiers. He's got altered Exceptionals in the mix."

"They are going to do what they can to come back in one piece." Warren spoke up from his seat.

"See? Listen to your dad." James kissed Annie's temple.

"You two ready?" Chance poked his head in the room.

"We're ready, Chief." James planted another kiss on Annie's lips.

Annie hugged James as tight as she could. Knowing he had to go out there and watching him do it were two entirely different things. "I'll see you soon. I love you."

"I love you too, Anne." James squeezed her hand and headed out the door.

"Love you, sis. Love you guys" Ethan hugged her tight and darted out the door behind James.

Every monitor in the room sprang to life. Code raced across them until each one settled into an image of the surrounding area. Another wave of calm from her mother filtered through the room. "Thanks Mom."

"Not just for you, Annie." Abby smiled at her. "This is the hard part. Yes, going up there and fighting is hard but staying behind and supporting is just as hard."

"Your Mom is right. Sitting here and watching your friends and loved ones possibly get hurt can be nerve-wracking. We were overseas for the last big fight, but poor Ariel had to watch as the bomb that killed Joe went off." Warren adjusted the wheelchair in front of the desk.

"The conference room is the first time I've seen her. Okay who am I kidding? That was the first time I've seen a few people, but is going up there a good idea? I didn't because I knew it would distract James. He would have been too worried about something happening to me." Annie leaned back against the desk.

"She's determined to be up there. Especially with this Kaliya person that Steele has been experimenting on having Joe's DNA." Abby shrugged, "I can't say if it's a good idea or not."

Warren reached out and took Annie's hand in his. "Annie, I know this is going to sound odd coming from me, but James knows what he's doing. He led most of the extraction teams. Including the one that brought you home to us. I hate to say it, but he was created for this. When Steele made Talisa create him, it was for war."

Annie looked down at her father's remaining hand holding hers. "I know. I'm just worried. We haven't had enough time together. Not just him. All of them."

Abby wrapped her arm around Annie's shoulders. "We're all worried. We can only hope that your brother throws a tornado up Steele's ass."

"Mom! I didn't need the mental image with that." Annie laughed.

"I'm glad I could make you laugh at a time like this." Abby hugged Annie to her.

"We're in position." Talisa's voice interrupted through the earbud.

"We are as well." Lucas' voice crackled through next.

"Same here. Anything on the monitors?" James' voice followed.

"Nothing yet. All quiet so far." Annie rubbed her hand along the back of her neck.

"Wait, Annie I think we have something. An old relay in Fort Peck is picking up chatter." Warren straightened up in his chair.

Annie did the calculations in her head and flipped through every camera angle they had. She pushed and accessed the cameras at Fort Peck. Several helicopters heading straight for them. "That's them guys. Ten minutes. Helicopters incoming.

"Copy that." Came through in unison from Talisa, James, and Lucas.

Charlotte stayed crouched down with her group. Ten minutes felt like ten years waiting for Steele to show up. It took her by surprise that none of her parents argued for her to stay below. Especially before Abby decided to stay back as medical personnel.

"You okay Charlotte?" Chance interrupted her thoughts.

"Peachy. Popsicle. Just waiting for the show to start." Charlotte grinned at him. "If they are that close, maybe Ethan should give them something to contend with."

James nodded in agreement, "She's right. Ethan let's hinder them on their approach. Anything with water will just add to what Lucas and Dad can use."

Ethan nodded and rolled his head from one side and then the other. His eye clouded over, and a clap of thunder boomed overhead.

Charlotte looked up at the sky as the clouds rolled in thick and dark. It would cut off some of their own visibility, but it would definitely make it harder for the helicopters coming towards them. Lightening steaked across the sky.

The trees ahead of them swayed with the wind that had picked up. Another crack of thunder and rain came down in the woods in front of them, but they remained dry. It amazed her how much control Ethan had gained over time. In the beginning he didn't even want to mess with it, but Ilana had encouraged him and now her brother-in-law had control that most people envied.

Whumpa-whumpa-whumpa-whumpa. The sound of the approaching helicopters echoed through the grove.

"Incoming, just south of your position. We're counting five currently and there may be a second wave." Annie's voice came through the communicator. *"Assuming that nasty storm is Ethan's doing?"*

"Yeah, sis that's me." Ethan stayed crouched down.

"Well, it's working. Two of them are pulling back to look for a better place to land. Going to assume one of those is Steele." Annie's voice crackled. *"Watch the intensity of the storm though. We don't want it to kill our communications."*

"Got it, sis. I'll keep an eye on it." Ethan grinned as another bolt of lightning shot across the sky.

"Dad, let's give them a little more trouble landing." Charlotte waggled her eyebrows. Deep down she knew she shouldn't be so excited to be in a fight like this, but she rarely displayed her animalistic side. Then again, she rarely got to use her plant talents for anything other than helping their crops grow or helping Chance burrow down to the next level they had been building.

"Focus, Charlotte." Chance smirked at her.

James pointed towards the first helicopter that came into view. "That one is looking for a place to land."

Charlotte grabbed Chance's hand and tapped into her plant ability. One of them would be able to do some damage. The two of them together should be able to take out that helicopter. Several trees in the grove shook underneath the helicopter. To any normal person they would think that the wind from the storm shook them.

Without warning the trees grew at an exponential rate. Two of them swung apart and came together as if killing a bug between two hands. In this case the bug was a helicopter. Flames shot out from the helicopter as it exploded. Even with the rain it would still catch the forest on fire.

Tapping into her ability to control fire she pulled it back as pieces of the wreckage hit the ground. War was one thing. A war in the middle of a forest fire was something completely different.

"Holy shit, sis." James looked at her impressed.

"Hey, that wasn't just me." Charlotte smiled at her brother.

"Effective, but not exactly non-lethal." Chance chided her.

Charlotte cringed, "Sorry, Dad."

Chance shook his head, "Don't apologize. I know I said let's try and stay non-lethal, but this is war. There are going to be casualties."

"We just don't want to be among those casualties." Ethan added.

"Exactly." Chance agreed.

"James there's weapons locked on your location. Watch out!" Warren's voice came through the earbuds.

Charlotte didn't hesitate to tap back into her gift. Roots shot out of the ground, forming a dome over them. The dome grew thicker and thicker by the second. The earth below them parted. Roots wrapped each of them in a cocoon and pulled them down. She heard her father and brothers yelp in surprise, but she didn't take the time to respond. Focusing on ensuring they were protected was her priority. The roots around them burrowed down fifty feet or so into the earth creating a pocket for them. The cocoons of roots around each of them receded.

The roots above them continued to fill in the space weaving an intricate shield. The missile hit, raining down soot and bits of fire towards them. With a quick switch of her gifts, she pulled the flames above out until there was nothing left but smoke.

The impact had knocked her off her feet. She beat at an ember on her sleeve that refused to go out. "Well, that was humbling."

"Fuck me, Shorty. Talk about quick thinking." James brushed the dirt off his hands.

"Don't thank me yet. We've got to get back up there." Charlotte swayed and grabbed onto Chance's hand when her father reached out for her.

"Easy, Charlotte. That was a lot of power you used." Chance hugged Charlotte to him and kissed the top of her head.

Crackles and static filtered through their earpieces. *"J…any..you.."*

"Think I might have taken us out of range. Ironic since Annie and them are further underground than we are right now." Charlotte squeezed Chance's hand. "I'm okay Dad."

Chance kept a hand on Charlotte's back. "I know you are. Take it easy for a minute. I'll work on getting us back up."

Roots shot out from the side of the hole Charlotte had pulled them into. They braided and intertwined into a floor. It spread out until it was big enough for the four of them to fit on it. Once the four of them were situated, it started to rise like an elevator.

"James! Ethan! Charlotte! Chance! Any of you! Are you there?" Annie's panicked voice came through the earpieces.

"We're good." Chance answered. "Thanks to some quick thinking by Charlotte."

"Oh, thank God!" Annie's voice sounded relieved. *"They've landed. You've got soldiers incoming."*

James twirled his knife in his hand. "Let's go then. They probably think they took us out with that shot."

"Then let's use that to our advantage." Charlotte got to her feet and pulled back the remains of the charred dome of vines, ready for whatever Steele threw at them next.

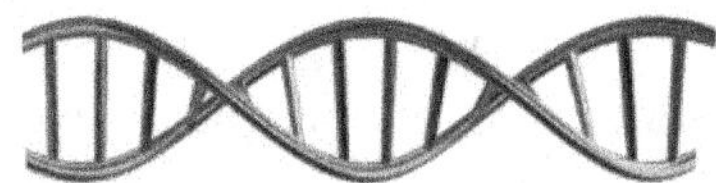

"What's the hold up? Why are we slowing down?" Steele glowered at the pilot. They should have been there already and destroying the Infected.

"There's a storm sir. We have to go slower to get through it."

"Go around it then. We're wasting time." Steele shook his head. No one else knew what it took to get rid of the Infected.

"Sir, the storm is several miles wide. It would take hours to go around it. We're almost there."

"Just get us there." Steele looked around at the occupants of the helicopter with him. His prized experiment sat stone still and straight up. Looking at it still unnerved him, but if it accomplished half of what Taylor promised, then it was worth it.

Suddenly the helicopter lurched to the side causing Steele to grab ahold of his seat. "What the hell was that?"

"Chopper one is down, sir." The pilot's voice came through his headphones.

"Down? What do you mean down?" How could they lose a chopper already? They hadn't even landed yet. That chopper had their initial troops in it.

"It's destroyed, sir. The trees destroyed it."

"What the fuck do you mean 'the trees destroyed it'? Trees don't destroy helicopters. There had to be a missile or something." Steele yelled at the pilot. How could he think that the trees destroyed a helicopter? Trees didn't attack things. Trees were stationary in the ground. The soldiers had to be seeing things.

"We read no attack or missile being fired, sir."

"You're fucking seeing things. Get us on the ground." Steele seethed from his seat. Everyone around him was incompetent.

"We're pulling back to land, so we don't get too close. Chopper three fired on a target but we can't see anything else through this rain."

"Get us on the fucking ground then before you get us all killed. Our secret weapon is on board. It needs to be in one piece." Steele focused on Kaliya. He hated to even think of *it* with an actual name. Even if it needed a name, why Taylor couldn't pick something more normal or American he had no idea. Every time he looked at it, he felt bile rise in his throat. With the alterations it looked more like a dragon or a lizard than a human.

"We're trying, sir. The wind is picking up." The pilot sounded annoyed.

"I don't care what you have to fucking do. Get us on the God damn ground. That is a fucking order." Steele beat his fist against the back of the pilot's seat. Spittle flew from his mouth, but he didn't care. These people needed to understand that he was in.

Kaliya said nothing, but one eyebrow rose the slightest bit.

"Do you have something to add to the conversation?" Steele glared at Kaliya. How dare it even react. Its only function was to obey orders and kill other Infected.

"No, General." Kaliya straightened up in her seat. The look on her face was no longer passive. She looked annoyed.

"Who asked you anyway? You are here to serve a purpose. Nothing more." Why did that thing keep staring at him? Taylor should have made it, so it only obeyed orders. That's why they grafted the DNA of a soldier. Not just for the power of regeneration.

The helicopter tossed from side-to-side on landing. "Don't you even know how to fly this thing?" Steele scoffed at the pilot. "Can't find good help anywhere."

Kaliya unbuckled from her seat the moment the helicopter touched down.

"Where the fuck do you think you're going? It's not time for you to go out there yet. You're our surprise." Steele sneered across the small space at it.

"I am suiting up General. I will not leave the helicopter until you give the order." Kaliya's eyebrow rose as if to challenge him to say something else.

Steele fought with the seatbelt to get it unhooked. He slammed himself back against the seat when Kaliya approached him. "What are you doing? Get back! You don't touch me. That's an order!"

Kaliya reached in and unhooked the seatbelt with two fingers. She immediately turned her back to him and went through a duffle bag.

"Well then." Steele cleared his throat in an attempt to hide his embarrassment. He definitely didn't want that thing touching him. "Your main orders remain the same. You are to kill every Infected that you see so we can eradicate them from the planet. I have a few side orders for you as well."

Kaliya turned around and stood at attention. "Yes sir. Your orders?"

A smile spread across his face. Steele flipped around a tablet with a picture of Talisa on it. "You find this one and you are to subdue her and bring her to me. We're going to bring her back in and see if we can't make her more compliant to do what I need her to do in the lab." His finger swiped left to reveal a picture of Roark. "Perhaps restrain Talisa and make her watch as you kill this one."

The expression on Kaliya's face stayed calm and even. Not even a hint that it was even listening to him.

"Are you paying attention?"

"Yes, General. Kill that one in front of Talisa. Subdue her and bring her to you. Were there any other Infected you wanted special attention paid to?" At least it stood at parade rest when it spoke to him.

"As a matter of fact, there is." Another swipe left revealed a picture of Ariel. "Something wrong?" Steele asked at the low rumble that filled the space in the back of the helicopter.

"Not at all General. Just anxious to get out there and carry out you orders."

"Good. Get ready. I should be getting reports back from the first encounters any minute and then we'll be ready to send you out there to do some damage." Steele shoved the tablet back in the pack he'd retrieved it from. "As soon as you have Talisa, you are to signal me, and I will meet you out there to bring my prize home."

Talisa crouched down next to Roark. Elan and Chaz close by them. They knew the storm that had come in had been Ethan's doing but it did hinder their field of vision. Despite their limited visibility she didn't have to ask who was responsible when a helicopter exploded between two trees.

"Shit." Roark's exclamation pulled her focus away from the fiery bits of helicopter and soldiers falling to the ground.

"Fuck." Talisa caught the missile that headed straight for their family.

"James! Ethan! Any of you!" Annie's panicked voice came through the earbud.

"Shit, sis." Elan blinked a few times and shook her head.

"Elan?" Talisa leaned towards her daughter. Even Chaz leaned in towards her with a quizzical expression.

"Whatever she did, Char used some power. They're not dead." Elan wiggled her finger in her ear. "Damn twin connection."

"James! Ethan! Charlotte! Chance! Any of you! Are you there?"

"We're good." Chance's voice crackled through the earpieces.

"Oh, thank God!" Annie's voice sounded relieved. *"They've landed. You've got soldiers incoming."*

"They're closest to you, Tal. Counting at least fifteen, but more choppers are trying to land." Warren's voice joined the conversation.

"We're on it." Talisa answered. "We see them coming."

"Looks like it's show time." Roark shifted his weight while rotating three spheres of water in his hand.

Chaz leaned in close to Roark's face. "No time for show. Time to fight."

Talisa chuckled, "He means it's time to fight. Those guys coming towards us are our targets. Left or right Elan?"

"Caiman." Elan growled at her.

"Left or right, Caiman." Talisa smirked at her daughter as she repeated the questions.

"Well take the right. Come on, Cheetah." Elan's skin thickened and her nails elongated.

Chaz for his part sped off and bounced off the closet soldier knocking him over, surprising the rest around them. A few stray bullets fired off around them.

"Ready lover?" Talisa flicked the lighter in her hand and pulled in a ball of fire letting it grow.

Roark grinned back at her. His own three spheres of water combining and growing in size to match her fire. "Play ball."

Both stood up and threw their respective elements at the group of soldiers. The pair that Roark hit were surrounded by the water and taken up towards the tops of the trees. He hung them up on the higher branches and left them there.

Talisa went with a different approach and kept a smaller ball of fire back to act like a remote control. As she twisted the flame in her hand around itself into a funnel, the group she was focused on spiraled high in a fiery tornado. Once they were up near the ones that Roark had stranded, she clenched her hand into a fist and extinguished the tornado with the soldiers still a hundred feet in the air.

"God, that was sexy." Roark grinned over at her.

Chaz blurred in between them and stopped short. A growl resonated between the two of them. "Fight now. Fuck later."

Roark chuckled, "We are fighting."

Chaz rolled his eyes and took off again towards another attacker. Elan sliced another two soldiers in half from her spot ahead of them.

"I guess we're behind." Talisa sighed. "There's more coming." She threw her hands out in front of her towards the bodies of the still burning bodies. The fire came towards her like an old friend. It wrapped around her and caressed her skin. A burst of flame to her right caught her attention.

"Get 'em Char." Talisa grinned as she watched Charlotte take out two soldiers by their group.

A bark-like yell came from her husband. No need to wonder what happened. One of the soldiers got a shot off near them and he'd been hit. Just like she had when they were escaping Steele.

Roark grabbed her soldier with tendrils of water and bashed them against the closest tree. He backed up towards her and gritted his teeth.

"You, okay?" Talisa set her hand over the wound to cauterize it.

A low growl rumbled between them. "Thanks, Li. I will be. Fucker caught me off-guard."

"Tal and Roark be careful. Steele has his sights set on you two. He's ordered Kaliya to kill Roark and take Tal." Ariel's voice came through the earpiece.

"Why am I not surprised? Have we figured out if we can trust her yet?" Talisa looked over the wound with a doctor's eyes for a moment. "You're going to have a scar lover."

"It will match yours." Roark shrugged and pushed a wall of water out from them at the next round of soldiers that came at them.

"It still feels like we can trust her, but I'll let you know if anything changes. Mother fuckers, get away from my daughter." Ariel sounded like she meant business with whomever decided to get near Mackenzie.

Two soldiers went flying over their heads and past the wall of water Roark had been using to contain some of the soldiers.

"Who decided it was a good idea to piss off the redhead?" Roark asked in the earpiece.

"It's been handled." Ariel stated matter of fact.

"Ready for more, lover?" Talisa watched Elan and Chaz take out three more between them.

"With you, Li? Always." The wall of water parted just enough for a few soldiers to get through.

"There's still more coming. Three at a time doesn't quite seem fair. They really have no chance." Talisa lifted one hand. A fireball shot out and hit one of the soldiers in the chest, exploding on impact.

A deluge of water came down on top of the now burning soldier and put him out. "Chance is going to be pissed at us if we don't drop at least a few of them into the pit."

"He's just going to have to be pissed at me then. This is war and Steele isn't trying to ground us. He's trying to kill us." Talisa threw out two more fireballs at the approaching group.

"I mean we have to at least try and not set the forest on fire. That would be bad." Roark threw a blast of water at one of the trees that had caught fire.

"Let's get rid of these assholes."

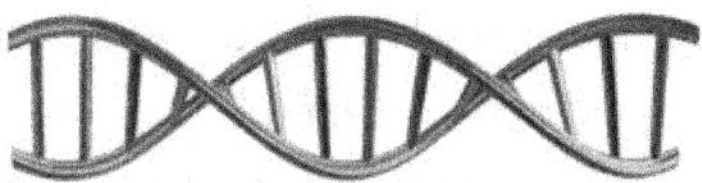

Kaliya stood by the open door of the helicopter. The rain came down in sheets making it nearly impossible to see anything. General Steele still sat in the same seat he had been in when they landed. Attempting to flip through images on the pad in his hand. Complaining that said images weren't loading fast enough. Not to mention that their attack wasn't going according to his plan.

With one hand she reached outside into the rain. The droplets that caressed her skin felt more calming than any breathing exercise Taylor would have told her to do. Ariel was out there. She could feel her. Their connection became stronger now that they were in the same area. No matter what orders the General had given her she wouldn't kill the other woman.

How could she follow any of the orders she had been given? The Infected…no…the Exceptionals that were out there fighting for their lives were Ariel's family. Technically speaking, from a scientific standpoint, she shared DNA with Ariel's daughters.

Kaliya flipped her hand over and wiggled her fingers against the falling water.

"What in the blazes are you doing?" Steele snapped her out of her mental musings.

224

"Awaiting your orders to attack, General." She didn't bother turning around to look at him.

"Playing in the rain while you wait? I swear Taylor gave you extra DNA but took away your damn common sense." Steele muttered.

"I'm gauging the best plan of attack. The rain is calming." Kaliya rolled her eyes knowing he couldn't see her do it.

"Calming? We're at war, you fucking idiot." Steele yelled back at her. "Stupid fucking defective Infected. Rain does not relax a soldier."

"Everything okay Ari?" The pitter-patter of the rain hit the top of the covered porch. Joe walked up behind Ariel. She leaned against the post wrapped up in a blanket, her hair piled on top of her head in a messy bun.

"Hey there, Tiger." Ariel flashed a smile over her shoulder at him. "Just restless. Everything is quiet on the monitors, so I came up to listen to the rain."

Joe took the blanket from her and pulled it around the two of them. He wrapped his arms around her waist and kissed the side of her neck. "Been awhile since we've been able to do that. Hell, half the time we only know it's raining because of the monitors."

Ariel intertwined her arms with his and snuggled back into him. "Exactly why I came up her."

"Why didn't you wake me up?" He nestled his chin on her shoulder.

"I thought about it because you always said that the sound of rain relaxes you. You guys had such a long day with that supply run that I thought you needed the sleep." Her hand came up and caressed the side of his face.

"I know, I'm weird." He shrugged and pulled the blanket around them a little tighter.

"No more than me. I love the smell of the rain. You remember that one safe house we stayed in? We listened to the rain on that tin roof all night."

Joe nuzzled the side of her neck with a chuckle. "That's not all we did that night."

Ariel giggled but didn't pull away. She turned in his arms to face him, "No, it definitely wasn't."

"I love you Ari."

"I love you too, Tiger."

The memory hit out of nowhere. Tears welled up in her eyes from it. She hoped Steele didn't notice her reverie.

"Are you even fucking listening to me, you Infected idiot?" Steele hollered at her.

"My apologies, General. I was listening to those attacking already. Forming a plan of attack based on what they are saying to get the maximum effectiveness for your orders." Shit, he had noticed. It would all be a lot easier if she just snapped his neck now. Wait a minute. Was that her thought? It felt like her thought, but it also felt very much like Joe did in the memory.

"Liya, are you okay? You feel very conflicted." Ariel's voice slipped into her brain like silk.

"I am well Ariel. I am conflicted. We are about to meet on a battlefield." She couldn't explain what had just happened yet. If they all survived this, then they could talk about it.

"I know. I'm not happy about it either. Please be careful." Ariel's worry came through clear as a bell.

"You as well. I will see you soon." The connection drifted away again until it was just the tingle at the base of her skull that Kaliya had become accustomed to.

"It is almost time for you to put whatever plan you have in your empty little head into action. You had better not fuck it up. Because if you do, I will make sure you are terminated with the rest of the stupid fucking Infected out there. You are all on borrowed time until we eradicate this godforsaken infestation as it is." Steele had finally left his seat and approached her. He actually had the audacity to get close to her as he leveled his threats against her.

"Yes General." Better not to engage with him. Did he even realize that he just told her that his plan included killing her once he finished using her? Probably not. Or maybe he just didn't care.

"Nothing to say to that hmm? That's right because Taylor gave me an empty vessel. Can you even carry out your orders?" Steele stood toe-to-toe with her now.

"Yes General." It would be so easy to just rabbit-punch this man in the face right now. Who cared about a court-marshal? If it shut him up it would be worth it.

"What is it?" Steele pressed his finger against the earbud in his ear. "I believe that's your signal. Do not fuck this up.

"Yes General."

Danny chased down the hallway after the most precocious little girl he had ever met. In fact, he was positive she was smarter than him. "Orenda, wait up. Where are ya goin' kiddo? We're supposed to be staying with everyone else."

"Come on. We're gonna be late." Orenda's dark curls bounced around her as she ran down the hallway.

"Late for what? We're supposed to be staying safe down here." Danny shook his head with a sigh. They hadn't talked about it yet, but he was pretty sure this little girl happened to be the one that Elan had talked to him about. His wife's daughter. His stepdaughter. Who thought it was a good idea to trust him with a kid?

"We can't miss it. Come on." Her little legs carried her through the compound faster than he thought possible for someone who had only been out of a coma for a few hours.

"Okay. We can't miss it. What can't we miss?" He finally caught up with her and scooped her up. A combination of a screech and a bunch of giggles erupted from the curly-haired child he now held in his arms. Danny flipped her around to face him in his arms. "All right little miss. Tell me where we're going, and I'll get us there *if* I think it's safe."

Her little eyebrow quirked up reminding him of her mother so much in that moment. There was no mistaking that Orenda was a Nashuk. She already had the attitude. "Daddy…can I call you Daddy? I mean you're my stepdad and all that, but you're *gonna* be my Daddy when Mom decides she can handle being around me."

Definitely smarter than him. How the hell did she know any of that? No one had even mentioned who her mother was or that she was related to anyone in the compound. At least not that he knew of. He had enough trouble trying to help Chaz, how the hell could he help raise a little girl that already proved she could run circles around him? "Uh…sure…I mean…yeah, that's fine."

"Okay. Daddy, we need to go see Aunt Illy. We need to watch her. I need to talk to her." His stepdaughter squirmed in his arms. "Can we go? We're gonna miss it."

The only thing Danny could do for a moment was blink. He stared at her and blinked. "Uh…yeah…" He set her on the ground, and she took off like a shot towards Ethan and Ilana's room. "Wait. How are you gonna talk to Illy? Isn't she in a cocoon or something?"

Orenda stopped on a dime and spun to face him. "It's a chrysalis. She's learning stuff and she needs to hurry."

"Why exactly does she need to hurry?" Danny caught up to her again and looked down at her. He almost burst out laughing at the exasperated look on her face when he asked the question. Her hands went to her hips, and she huffed out a breath like he'd annoyed her.

"Um, well, Gramps got shot, but Grams burned him to help. Aunt Kenzie's mom got shot and hurted too. Uncle James got stabbed. Yeah, she needs to hurry before it gets bad." Orenda turned and started down the hallway again as if she hadn't just dropped that revelation on him.

"Orenda, how do you know all of that?" Dumfounded. There was no other word for it.

"Uma told me." She skipped off down the hallway.

"Fuck me." Danny rubbed his temples for a moment. He shook his head at the realization that he should probably watch his mouth since he was with a six-year-old.

Orenda giggled and skipped down the hallway until she reached the door. "Daddy, hurry up! I can't reach the button. This place is not made for short people."

Danny bit the inside of his cheek to keep from laughing. There would definitely be a talk with his mother-in-law when this was all over. Talisa left him in charge of his stepdaughter that not only was smarter than him, but she also talked to their ancestors. He walked up to the door and punched in the code for the door to open. Orenda took off the second the door opened, and he followed behind her. "Orenda be careful. We don't know what's going on."

Orenda turned and tilted her head to the side with the same look of exasperation. "I do. She's learning and changing." She poked the cocoon. "Hurry up, Aunt Illy. They're gonna need you real soon."

Danny covered his mouth to keep himself from saying something stupid. He stood there and watched a six-year-old little girl talk to this cocoon or chrysalis or whatever it was like a person stood in front of her. That's when things got weird. The cocoon on the couch was there and then suddenly it wasn't. It phased in and out of existence. Without thinking he scooped up Orenda and stepped back from the couch. If anything happened to her Talisa would kill him.

"It's okay, Daddy. She's learning." Orenda wrapped her arms around his neck.

"So, that's supposed to be happening?" He pointed to the still phasing object on the couch.

Orenda nodded emphatically. "Yup. She's dreamin' and when she doesn't get it, it starts all over." She looked over at the couch again. "Come on, Aunt Illy. You can do it. It's gettin' bad out there. The bad man is comin' to get Grams."

"Wait, what? Steele is comin' to get Talisa?" At Orenda's nod he looked between the couch and the little girl in his arms.

"Then your Aunt Illy needs to get a move on huh?"

"Yes sir, she does." She nodded somberly.

"Cover your ears little miss." When she complied with the biggest grin on her face, he shifted his gaze to the couch. "Ilana get your ass in gear. This has gone on long enough. Learn what ya gotta learn and get yer ass out there to help your husband and the rest of our family."

"Kenzie behind you!" Ariel called out a split second before a blast of water shot from behind her to take out the soldier advancing on Mackenzie.

"Thanks, Lucas. Where the hell do they keep coming from? It's like they're never ending!" Mackenzie leaned over with her hands on her knees to catch her breath.

"They landed in several areas, so they are coming at us from all sides." Lucas moved to his wife's side.

"Base, how are we looking on incoming?" Ariel asked in the earpiece.

"First wave looks like it's petering out. Second wave is gearing up and if what you said earlier is true, this is going to be his big guns." Warren answered.

Ariel rolled her neck from side-to-side. "Just what we wanted. Shit. Ground!"

The trio hit the ground as a hail of bullets whizzed over them. A wall of water surrounded them and pushed out enough for them to stand back up.

"Thanks, Lucas." Ariel nodded in her son-in-law's direction.

"There are several Exceptionals headed in our direction that are not from our compound." Lucas pointed to the south. One of the advantages of being telepathic. When you've been around each other as long as this group had, you learned their mental signatures.

Ariel looked up at the trees that had grown earlier in the fight. It looked like Roark had been hanging soldiers up there like Christmas ornaments. A few had tried to get down and unfortunately fallen to their death or been impaled on the branches on the way down.

Another group of soldiers approached them. It started to look like a choreographed dance between the three of them. A burst of water here or there. A water shield thrown up to protect them from bullets, then wrapping around the soldier and tossing them away from them. Hers and Mackenzie's telekinesis shielding them or shoving the soldiers away. For the most part, it kept them from getting too close to them.

"Fuck." Ariel jerked back and landed on the ground. Her arm felt like it was on fire. Her shield didn't catch all the bullets and one must have hit her. At least it hadn't hit Mackenzie or Lucas.

"Mom!" Mackenzie stopped immediately and ran to her side. "Where are you hit?"

"Kenzie, watch out!" Ariel getting hit started a chain reaction.

Mackenzie knelt next to her and didn't see the soldier coming from behind her. Ariel threw up her other arm and threw him back.

"Mom, where are you hit?" Mackenzie attempted to coax the answer out of her.

"My arm. I'll live. We'll worry about it later. We're about to get overrun if we don't get back up." Ariel pushed on the ground with her good arm coupled with her gift and her daughter to get her on her feet.

None of them had time to react to the soldier that tackled Mackenzie to the ground. Ariel was knocked to the side and fell back to the ground.

"Mackenzie!" Lucas spun around while throwing a wave of water behind him to keep the other soldiers at bay.

Ariel turned her head in his direction a spilt second before a large being dove through the wave and tackled the soldier off Mackenzie. She scrambled to her feet and held Lucas back. "Wait."

"Ariel!" Lucas' insistent voice slammed into her brain.

"Kaliya. She won't hurt Kenzie…or me." Ariel answered in a gentle tone.

"Are you sure?"

"Mostly."

"That is not comforting." Lucas sighed mentally.

Kaliya rolled with the soldier and snapped his neck before she stood up. A thick wall of water surrounded them. Their new addition raised an eyebrow.

"Kenzie are you okay?" Ariel motioned for Lucas to join her.

"I just got the wind knocked out of me. You, on the other hand are still bleeding." Her daughter smirked at her.

Ariel pulled at the torn fabric of her sleeve. "I'll be fine. They just winged me."

"Ari, you're injured?" Kaliya pulled the fabric aside with a frown. "It appears they just creased you. It will probably scar, but it is not life threatening."

Mackenzie took Lucas' hand to help her up. "Thank you for the help. Not to sound rude, but who are you?"

"My name is Kaliya." She offered Mackenzie a smile with a small bow.

"We can worry about introductions later. Lucas' wall of water is only going to hold up for so long." Ariel tore a strip of fabric from the bottom of her shirt to tie around her injury.

"That's not mine, Ariel." Lucas looked pointedly at Kaliya.

Kaliya took the strip of fabric from Ariel and dressed the wound as best they could in the field. "It's mine. Well, it's mine on top of what Lucas initially put up."

Ariel took Kaliya's hand and squeezed it. "Thank you. We have to figure out a way to end this."

"Steele ordered me to kill you and Roark and kidnap Talisa. I'm supposed to signal him to meet me when I have Talisa."

"Tal, we need you and Roark to make your way over to the giant water bubble please." Ariel said out loud and telepathically to Talisa and Roark. She mentally connected the group in front of her so they could hear the conversation.

"What's up Red?" Roark grunted in reply.

"If you aren't too busy, at the moment, I think we've got a way to draw Steele out and end this. If you're up for it that is."

Ariel met Kaliya's eyes hoping the trust she felt in the woman was justified.

"Sure, let me just finish my tea and crumpets." Roark quipped back.

"We're on our way, Ariel." When Talisa responded she swore she could feel the woman rolling her eyes at her own husband.

"What are you thinking, Ariel?" Lucas folded his arms across his chest.

"I'm thinking that once they are over here Kaliya should tell Steele he has what he wants and get him to come over here so we can have a little chat." Ariel grinned at her companions.

"I don't know what Ariel's got planned, but something tells me it's going to be interesting." Roark threw a wave of water at a group of soldiers, sending them flying.

A burst of fire went off next to him from Talisa as they made their way towards the giant bubble of water. "I'm sure you're right. She sure came out guns blazing when she decided she was done wallowing."

"Still not sure if we should trust this Kaliya person, no matter what Red says. Is she just trusting her because she has a small piece of Joe's DNA?" They alternated throwing fire and water at the enemy soldiers as they made their way to the water enclosure.

"We'll find out soon enough. Either way if we have a chance to get rid of Steele, we need to take it." Talisa stopped at the edge of the dome.

Roark took her hand and wrapped them in a bubble of water. He pushed through to the other side where the others were gathered. The water fell away from them and revealed three of their own and the newcomer who didn't look more than human. Not that it was an issue. There were plenty of

Exceptionals that had taken on animalistic traits. "What's the plan, Red?"

Ariel rolled her eyes with a smile. "Straight to the point. Guess that makes sense since we are in the middle of a battle." She gestured towards Kaliya, "Tal…Roark, this is Kaliya." Then she gestured to them in turn, "Kaliya, this is Talisa and Roark. They are Lucas' parents so Kenzie's in-laws."

"What's with the family tree Ariel?" Roark pushed his thoughts directly to Ariel not wanting to offend the newcomer right off the bat.

Ariel didn't waste any time with her answer. *"Short version. She's protective of me, Kenzie, and Tori along with our families. I'm making sure the familial connections are established."*

"Appreciate it." Roark folded his arms across his chest, looking very similar to Lucas. "So, what is the plan?"

Kaliya spoke up this time. "Steele tasked me with subduing Talisa and killing Roark in front of her along with killing Ariel."

Ariel continued, "So now that you are both here, Kaliya can contact him to have him join us so he…"

"Wait a minute." Roark cut her off. Did they just ask them to join them just to hand them over?

"Let her finish, lover." Talisa nudged him.

"Sorry Ariel."

"It's fine. I know how it sounds." Ariel smiled over at him. "Kaliya offers for him to come watch her kill you in front of Tal. When he gets here, we have a few options."

Roark pinched the bridge of his nose. Lucas and Kenzie weren't arguing with her, so it probably wasn't the worst plan in the world. "And those options are?"

Lucas took over with the explanation. "Option one is for Ariel, Mom, and I to make him believe that's what he's actually seeing happen by projecting into his mind with our combined telepathy. A little tricky since we've never done anything like that before separate or together."

Kenzie took a turn, "Option two is we capture him and throw him in one of the containment cells."

"And finally, there's option three which is my preference," Ariel continued, "One of us snaps his neck. I'd like to be the one that does it but I'm willing to draw straws.",

Roark bit the inside of his cheek as he watched Kaliya shake her head behind Ariel when the other woman said she would like to be the one that did it. The newcomer did have a vested interest in Ariel. "Capture doesn't really seem like the best idea. I mean, it's the most peaceful, but in the long run it's not going to change anything."

"Roark's right and while at some point I think the three of us should practice an option one type of scenario, now is not the time to try something like that for the first time." Talisa weighed in while looking over Ariel's arm and offering a smile and nod to Kaliya.

Kaliya held up her finger to the group. "General Steele. I have them subdued. If you can meet me, you can observe as I kill them. Yes sir. I await your arrival." She lowered her finger.

"I guess we agree that it's going to be option three." Roark chuckled. Kaliya definitely had a straightforward attitude.

"If you have three options and two are eliminated that only leaves the remaining option. Why would we hesitate? Other than who will have the honors, there isn't much left to discuss." Kaliya looked at him as if he'd grown another head.

Talisa touched her earpiece, "Base, we need a message sent out. Steele is coming to the giant water dome. Do not engage. Let him pass."

238

"Copy. Groups one and three, Steele is on the move do not engage." Annie's voice came through.

"Ma, what the fuck? Tell me you aren't making a deal with that asshole." James' angry voice came through.

Roark answered using his own earpiece. "I'm with your mother, son. No deal is being made. This ends today. Do as you are told and do not engage."

"We copy. Whatever you're doing, Spirts be with you." Chance put an end to any ensuing argument.

"Are you fucking kidding me? You're going to get yourself killed." Elan's voice burst into his ear loud and angry.

Elan's answer worried Roark. He had to hope that she and Chaz would listen. "Yes, Caiman. We know what we are doing. I promise." He pinched the bridge of his nose again. There he was, standing under a dome of water, arguing with his children about how to deal with a homicidal maniac.

"He will be here in less than ten minutes. Once I let him into the dome, his guards will need to be dealt with." Kaliya stood behind Ariel but stayed close to her. Closer than you would expect for having just met face-to-face.

"Got it. Throw the guards back with the other ones we tossed off." Kenzie leaned against Lucas.

Roark watched the proud expression Kaliya had on her face as she looked at Mackenzie. The whole situation was…surreal. "Get rid of guards, kill the maniac. Got it. What could go possibly wrong?"

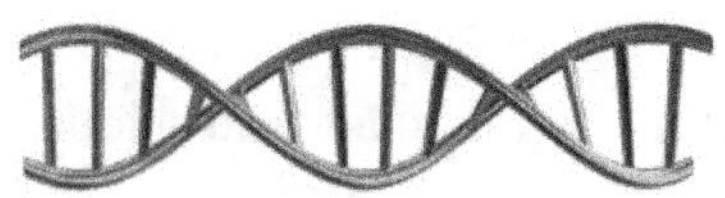

Ilana reached for the clouds as she had a thousand times since she had been wrapped up in the cocoon. Each time it ended with her body broken and bloody. Each time more painful than the last. This time as she floated on her back, when she felt the familiar tug of the string on her ankle Ethan's voice echoed in her head. *"What if you had faith in yourself and you didn't fall?"*

"It wasn't me. It was Steele. I did what I could."

The string disintegrated, falling to the ground like ash. For the first time in longer than she could remember, a genuine smile spread across her face. No wings sprouted from her back, but she took off towards the clouds. She soared through the sky letting the wind caress her face.

Ilana stopped on a dime and hovered in one spot. One look at the chestnut brown skin on her hands told her that her natural form had taken over. The form she once likened to a Skinwalker. In this instance, it didn't bother her. It was a part of her. Ethan had always told her that, but she had never listened.

A whisper on the wind reached her ears. Ethan? No Danny's voice.

"Ilana get your ass moving. This has gone on long enough. Learn what ya gotta learn and get yer ass out there helping your husband and the rest of our family." Danny's muffled voice reached her.

Shit. Steele. The majority of her family had been fighting Steele and his soldiers while she had been learning. She had to get out there and help. Her eyes fell shut and she inhaled a deep breath. When she turned toward the ground and started straight for it no fear crossed her mind. A couch with a cocoon appeared on the ground.

When she made contact her perspective flipped. The sky and clouds disappeared. Everything went dark. Ilana was inside the cocoon. She stretched out and broke a hand through it. Muffled from the other side she heard a little girl's voice.

"Daddy, she's coming!"

Little girl? But the only little girl she knew of in their area of the compound resided in the lab. Wasn't that little girl in a coma? Ilana pushed with her other hand and pulled at the sticky fibers that surrounded her.

"We can't help her Daddy. She has to do it herself."

"Wouldn't it go a lot faster if we helped her though?" Danny asked, confused.

"I don't make the rules."

Wait. Danny. Daddy? How long had she been gone? When did Elan and Danny have a kid? The questions only made her pull harder until she freed her head and shoulders. A quick turn of her head located Danny and the little girl. Dark curly hair.

"Aunt Illy!" The little girl squealed her name with glee.

"Can we help her now, little miss?" Danny smirked at the girl in his arms. He set her down on the ground and moved towards the couch. "How can I help, Ilana?"

"I…uh…" Something nagged at the back of her mind. She knew this little girl from somewhere. Yes, it was the girl that had been in a coma, but from somewhere else. The lightbulb went off in her head. Before the last huge battle. When she meditated, she would speak to her. "Orenda?"

"You remember!" Orenda launched herself at the couch and threw her arms around Ilana.

"Easy, little miss. Give Illy a minute." Danny tugged at bits of the cocoon to get it off of her legs.

Ilana hesitated for a moment, startled by Orenda's enthusiasm. She wrapped her arms around the little girl and hugged her tight. "I missed you."

Orenda shrugged. "I missed you too. You stopped listening." She rolled her eyes, "Adults never listen."

Danny chuckled, "So yeah…she's smarter than me. I'm screwed."

"You are so pretty like this." Orenda grinned at her.

At that moment Ilana realized she had come out of the cocoon in her natural form. Danny hadn't said anything about it being different.

"She's right. You are beautiful like this Illy." Danny's grin matched Orenda's

Ilana stared at her brother-in-law and blinked a few times.

"I've been doing that blinking thing a lot in the last hour." Danny held his hand out to her to help her up. "Easy. You've been out for a few hours."

Ilana glanced down at Orenda and hesitated again in an attempt to figure out how to ask the questions she wanted to ask. "How's it going up there?"

"A few injuries. We've lost about a dozen of our fighters so far." Danny scooped Orenda back up.

"Danny! Shouldn't we, you know, sugarcoat it a little bit." Ilana stared intently at him as she not-so-subtly inclined her head towards their little companion.

"About that. She's the one that told me who's been hurt because your Uma told her." Danny smirked back at her.

Ilana rubbed her forehead. "O-kay. Who's hurt?"

"Gramps got shot, but Grams burned him to help. Aunt Kenzie's mom got shot and hurted too. Uncle James got stabbed. The new lady helped Aunt Kenzie." Orenda gave the injury report with the same straight face she had when she had given it to Danny earlier.

"See what I mean?" Danny's smirk didn't change as he scooped Orenda back up.

"New lady?" Ilana looked between her brother-in-law and her niece.

"Fu…fudge if I know." The look on Danny's face when he caught himself was comical.

"I guess we'll find out soon enough." Ilana sighed. "Danny?"

Danny looked towards the door as if he was listening to something. His eyes went wide, and his mouth hung open a little bit. "Uh…"

Orenda reached out and closed Danny's mouth. "You're gonna catch flies like that, Daddy."

Ilana covered her mouth to stifle a giggle. "What's going on, Danny?"

He pointed to his ear, "Annie just ordered that they let Steele pass. He's on his way to your parents' location now."

"What the heck?" Ilana's eyes widened. What the hell were her parents doing? They just got away from that maniac not too long ago.

Danny adjusted his hold on Orenda. "I'm gonna see if I can find this one something to eat. You better get out there." He leaned down and kissed her forehead. "Good to have you back, sis. Be careful."

"See you guys soon." Ilana ran for the door to go join the fight.

Kaliya stood behind Ariel. It took every ounce of restraint to not touch the woman in front of her. The urge baffled her. They had established that the connection between them existed despite the unorthodox way it started, but this feeling went beyond that. Even looking at Mackenzie triggered a protective response in her. Her daughter. No. Joe and Ariel's daughter.

"You, okay?" Ariel laid her hand on top of Kaliya's.

"I am fine. Just waiting for the General to arrive. He should be her any minute." Kaliya smiled down at Ariel, despite the sick feeling in her stomach. Even if the plan they discussed worked they would need a few minutes where the General thought she remained on his side. Assurance that she still followed orders.

"So, who gets the honor?" Roark asked the question that Kaliya didn't want to answer.

"I've already volunteered for it, if no one else wants it." Ariel answered him. "We've all got reason to want to do it though."

"Mom, are you sure? Daddy wouldn't have wanted you to." Mackenzie attempted to sway her mother away from it.

Ariel moved over to her daughter and cupped her cheek. "Your father would have been worried because killing someone can change you. He's not wrong, but I'm pretty sure a few of those soldiers we tossed through the forest didn't survive."

Talisa raised her hand, "I don't mind doing it either. But let's see what happens when he gets here."

"He's here." Kaliya stated matter of fact. "I'm sorry."

"Sorry?" Lucas looked up at Kaliya confused.

The water parted to let Steele in the bubble. Kaliya yanked Ariel towards her and pressed a knife against her throat. "General." She inclined her head towards the man as he entered.

"Mom!" Mackenzie attempted to rush towards them, but Lucas held her back.

"Fuck me!" Roark flung his hand to the side. A wave of water hit the two soldiers with Steele and threw them out of the dome.

"Well, well. If it isn't my favorite Infected scientists." Steele pointed towards Kaliya. "I see it can follow orders. It even brought me some bonus Infected to kill."

Ariel struggled against Kaliya's grip. "You asshole."

"Such language. How did your Infected soldier ever tolerate it?" Steele stood there proud as a peacock.

Kaliya felt drops of water hit the arm she had wrapped around Ariel. It took her a moment to realize it had been Ariel's tears. "I am ready when you are, General."

"Let her go, Steele. You know it's us you want." Roark attempted to bargain with the General.

"Let's be honest Roark. I really only need Talisa. Once I have her memory wiped again, she'll do whatever I want." Steele grinned like a Cheshire cat at the group.

Without warning Steele lifted off the ground and was forcefully held suspended against the nearest tree. "Put me down. I command you to put me down."

"I don't need to touch you to kill you, mother fucker." Ariel shouted through her tears.

"Kill that bitch already." Steele yelled at Kaliya.

"Go ahead and kill me. It's still four against two. Talisa can turn you into barbecue before you hit the ground." Ariel continued her struggle against Kaliya's grip.

A sonic boom startled the group. The dome of water crashed down around them. A blur streaked across the sky. Soldiers in the general vicinity all laid down their weapons and started to scatter.

"Get back here. That's an order. Kill the Infected. Where are you going?" Steele yelled from his perch against the tree. None of the soldiers listened to him.

A spout of water hit Kaliya in the chest knocking her backwards. The grip she had on Ariel didn't loosen and they both went flying. They hit a tree and bounced off it. The knife in her hand went flying.

Whatever had streaked across the sky circled and landed in front of them. A female shaped being stepped forward. Her brown skin glistened in the sun that now came out from behind the parting clouds.

Kaliya shot to her feet and put herself between Ariel and the woman. Did Steele have another secret weapon she didn't know about? The ruckus had caused Ariel to break her concentration and Steele had fallen to the ground. They had to keep him from escaping, but she needed to protect Ariel and Mackenzie from the new variable.

"Get away from Ariel." The woman took a step towards them.

"Ilana wait!" Lucas moved towards the new player.

"Wait? She had a knife to Ariel's throat." Ilana glanced towards Steele and vines shot out of the ground. They grabbed the man and wrapped around him and the tree holding him there.

"A ruse." Kaliya stood up and helped Ariel to her feet and examined her throat. "I would not hurt Ariel or any of her family."

Ariel nodded with a shaky breath. "Kaliya wouldn't hurt me." She squeezed Kaliya's hand. The woman Kaliya had grown to admire stormed over to Steele and punched the man in the face.

"Baby girl?" Roark stepped forward. "You're okay."

"Um, not that I'm complaining, but why are all the soldiers leaving?" Mackenzie stepped up beside Lucas.

"Get back here you cowards. You Infected loving cowards!" Steele yelled behind them.

A vine snaked up and wrapped around his mouth to shut the man up. "I flew overhead and removed the mental programming from them. Steele had been brainwashing them all. Every single one of them had some sort of trigger. They're all gone now though." Ilana hugged her parents.

"You are beautiful like this, baby." Talisa hugged her daughter.

Kaliya wrapped her arm around Ariel as the woman leaned into her, "We still need to deal with the asshole." The woman in her arms stated the obvious.

"No, it appears that we don't." Mackenzie stated as she pointed over at the man tied to the tree.

"I took care of him." Ilana shrugged. "We should probably clean up this mess. The neighborhood is a disaster.

Just like that, it was over. No more Steele. No more experiments. Kaliya looked at the group in front of her. Nowhere for her to go.

Ariel smiled up at her, "Come on. Let's go home."

"Home?" Kaliya looked down at her confused.

"Yes. Home." Ariel wrapped her arm around Kaliya's waist. They followed the group back towards the tunnels.

Home. With the Exceptionals. No longer called Infected. Or it. Just home.

Epilogue

In the last year since Steele's demise, things had changed significantly. For the most part, everyone lived above ground now. There were still a few holdouts, but they remained a part of the community. Each unit had been given one of the houses topside. Some families stayed together in the bigger houses. Most of the residents attempted to return to some form of normalcy.

Trading still existed and not just amongst themselves, but with other communities as well. Steele's war had destroyed the country's infrastructure. Not to mention any use of the former currency system.

One glance at the clock put a smile on her face. Annie finished setting the table. It took a substantial amount of bartering with their ration tickets, but it was worth it. When James came home from his meeting with Chance, she could give him the good news. It didn't hurt that there was enough for them to eat for a week. Loaves of bread lined one counter to be distributed later. The room smelled heavenly.

"Anne?" James slammed the front door of the house and stormed into the living room. Did the meeting with Chance not go well?

The timer on the oven beeped at the same time as he came in. She pulled it out and set the roasting pan on the stove. With a flick of her wrist, she tossed the potholder on the counter and met him in the living room. "How did your meeting go?"

His lips met hers in a cursory kiss, nothing like she had expected with all the work he had been caught up in for the last few months. Getting everyone moved and settled had taken quite a bit of time. "Do I look like it went okay? You know damn well why I'm upset."

"I do?" Annie turned on her heel and strode right back into the kitchen.

"So, you're just going to walk away from this?" James' voice chased behind her.

"I'm not walking away, James. I'm going to finish getting dinner together. You are welcome to come with me and we can continue this conversation." Without waiting to see if he followed, she pulled some butter and a bowl with salad out of the refrigerator.

There were definite advantages to having their gifts while they rebuilt their lives. Chance and Charlotte made sure there were plenty of fresh vegetables. Not just in the fields that had been plowed, but in the hydroponics section down below.

When James entered the room after only a slight hesitation, his mouth dropped open. "Where did all of this come from?"

"Same place all of our food comes from." Whatever happened in his meeting with Chance must have short-circuited his brain.

"Anne!" He spun around to take everything in. "There's a huge roast, which smells amazing by the way. One, two, three,"

He pointed to each loaf of bread cooling on the counter. "Did I count that right? Twelve loaves of bread! What are we going to do with that much bread?"

A smile tugged at the corner of her lips. She grabbed two of the loaves of bread and started for the front door. "I did a little bartering."

"Where are you going now?" The doorbell rang.

Annie pulled the door open with a smile for Lucas standing on the other side. "Do you mind dropping one of these off with your parents?"

Lucas grinned back at her. "I do not mind at all." He held up a large pouch. "As requested, my dear. We thank you. Mackenzie has been busy and unable to bake."

"I bet she is. There's been an influx of births in the last few months." Annie grinned at him. Mackenzie had definitely put her midwife training to use since the war ended. "Happy to help. Let me know when it runs out and I'll make some more."

A low growl reverberated behind them. James hated being out of the loop. "What is going on here?

"Annie was kind enough to offer to bake some bread for the family." Lucas' eyes darted between the couple. He knew his brother well enough to know when it was a good time to make an exit. "I'll let you get back to your evening."

"Have a good night." She watched Lucas' retreating form for a moment and shut the door. "Why don't we back up and you tell me what's got you so riled up, hmm?"

"I don't even know what's going on in my own home."

"James," Annie cupped his cheek and pressed a soft kiss to his lips, "What happened in your meeting?

"My meeting?" James jerked his head back. "How could you? How could you tell Chance you would do it? You can't go."

"Wait. That's what's got your panties all twisted?" Annie pressed her lips together in a thin line. She walked back into the kitchen. Maybe if she carved up the roast, she wouldn't want to kick his ass. Couldn't go? She most certainly could go and he couldn't stop her.

"It's too dangerous."

Annie focused directly on the meat and potatoes in front of her. "Chance asked me, and I said yes. I don't know why you are so upset about this."

"I just said. It's too dangerous."

"Well, you don't get to tell me what I can and can't do. They need someone to read the computers to make sure they aren't bullshitting us when we're trading. Ilana and Ethan are going. Hell, your mom is going too since your dad is in Washington. My dad isn't up for it. Well physically he is but we still working on the mental side." She transferred enough meat for them to eat that night onto a plate and put the rest in a storage container.

"I still think it's too dangerous. I'll be on a separate mission. I can't watch your back." The tension in his voice vibrated against her back.

With her eyes closed she took a deep breath and let it out slowly. That's when she felt it through their mate bond. Fear. Not something he would ever admit. She set the knife down and wiped her hands on the towel. When she turned around, she could see the emotions she had felt from him in his eyes. "James, look at me."

His arms encircled her waist. "I can't lose you."

Annie wrapped her arms around his neck. "I'm right here. But you can't suffocate me. We're in the middle of trying to rebuild this country. We all have to pitch in. If that means that I'm running the computer stuff here then fine, but it also means that if they need me on a mission outside of the compound then I have to go. We need the medicine they have."

"But I won't be there."

"Exactly." She led him to a nearby chair and gave him a gentle push to sit down. Once he did, she perched on his lap. "You would be too focused on me to do what you need to do. Doesn't mean we won't ever go on a mission together, but I agree with Chance that we need to be on separate ones to start."

James pulled her close with a frustrated sigh, "I don't like it."

"Noted."

"I won't survive if something happens to you."

"Just like I won't survive if something happens to you, but we have to take those chances so we can survive with this new way of life."

"Why does our kitchen look like a bakery?" A total change of subject.

A soft laugh filled the space between them, "I did some bartering. Lucas and Kenzie gave me tea for the bread. Ethan gave me a bottle of Shine for two loaves. Something about making your sister French Toast. Ariel and Kaliya gave me the potatoes. Danny gave me a few ration tickets and Mom gave me flour."

"And dinner?"

"A loaf of bread and the extra ration tickets helped me get the roast from your parents from the pig they just slaughtered. We'll have meat to eat all week and I even have some bacon in the freezer. Oh, and Charlotte gave us some ice cream. I wanted to surprise you."

"Because?"

The confused look on James' face caused a loud abrupt laugh to escape. "Because I got good news today."

"And I came home and killed the mood, huh?" At least he looked apologetic when he said it.

"Why did you want to surprise me?" Back to the confusion again.

"Well, your mom and Charlotte took a look at all my blood work and when we are ready…we can start a family."

James' eyes widened, "Wait. You mean?"

"Everything is perfect."

His lips captured hers in a searching kiss. When he pulled back, he tucked a lock of hair behind her ear. "I love you, Anne."

"I love you too James."

About the Authors

Sarah Cass's world is regularly turned upside down by her three special-needs kids and loving mate, so she breaks genre barriers, dabbling in horror, straight fiction, and urban fantasy. An ADD tendency leaves her with a variety of interests that include singing, dancing, crafting, cooking, and being a photographer. She fights through the struggles of the day, knowing the battles are her crucible and though she may emerge scarred, she's also stronger. While busy creating worlds and characters as real to her as her own family, she leads an active online life with her blog, *Redefining Perfect*, which gives a real and sometimes raw glimpses into her life and art.

~

Mary Terrani lives a chaotic life as a wife and mother of two boys of the twenty-something. They keep her on her toes on a regular basis, so she's happy to get lost in other worlds. Her long-standing passion for the written word drives her need to create chaos with her pen that only she can solve. She loves to dabble in many genres, from young adult to paranormal, and post-apocalyptic piece she's co-written with fellow author, Sarah Cass.

When she's not writing, Mary can be found in a variety of activities including knitting, gaming, and anything involving her favorite geekdoms. Mom, author and all-around geek, she loves spending time with her family. You can find Mary on Instagram, Facebook and her website.

Books by Mary Terrani

Decking the Halls

The Exceptionals
Escaping Humanity
Chaos Theory

Books by Sarah Cass

The Tribe Series
The Tribe
The Wolf
The Chief
The Raven
The Dominion Falls Series
Changing Tracks
Derailed
Dark Territory
Runaway Train
Home Signal
The Lake Point Series
Santa, Maybe
Deep-Fried Sweethearts
Stalled Independence
Witch Way
A Thorough Thanksgiving
Eve's New Year
Heartstrings & Hockey Pucks
Luck of the Cowgirl
Stars, Stripes & Motorbikes
Free Falling
Love for Hire
Haunted Hearts
Stand Alone Novels
Masked Hearts
Leap

Divine Roses Ink

DivineRosesInk.com

www.ingramcontent.com/pod-product-compliance
Lightning Source LLC
Chambersburg PA
CBHW070450200726
48293CB00007B/2151